I0701632

Preludes & Apocrypha, Vol. I

©2023 by Varsity Aesthetics LLC

www.varsityaesthetics.com
www.littlewerewomen.com

Table of Contents

To those who have sought refuge from hatred
in the small, quiet, and forgotten places

To those who have been hunted
for the sake of their skins

To those who have dared
to defy the hunter

And to those who
follow the path
all the way to
the very end

**These stories
are for
you**

Octavius & Sons, Inc.
17 Elysium Street – Boston

September 25th, 1906

Ladies, Gentlemen, and Respected Wolf-Persons:

Octavius & Sons, Inc. (*est.* 1765) is pleased to bring you the inaugural issue of *Preludes & Apocrypha*. In an unusual departure from our thrilling catalog of academic journals like *Beginner's Advanced Ætherics* and *Elizabethan Wigs Weekly*, this new quarterly publication will be solely devoted to the exotic cultural traditions of the 'non-humans,' i.e., the werewolves or wolf-men.

This literary experiment has been lead by none other than celebrated Lupine authoress, Miss Josdarama March. Her award-winning works "The Anatomist" and "Talons Out! A Play in Ten Acts" have achieved widespread acclaim. Now, she brings the ancient lore of her mysterious species to a wider audience.

Many of my colleagues were taken aback at the announcement of our new publication. Some expressed alarm at this 'risky decision' and a few even had the gall to suggest it could ruin us. Nonsense! Octavius & Sons, Inc. (*est.* 1765) was founded on boldness. My great-grandfather, L. Philomon Octavius put it best when he penned our motto:

"Truſt & Fearleſſ Truthſ Printed at Rocke-Bottom Priceſ, Expir'd Couponſ and Flemiſh Currency Not Accepted."

In that spirit, we thank you for your bold, non-refundable subscription and sincerely hope you enjoy *Preludes & Apocrypha*.

Charles Octavius, Sr.
Publisher

Foreword

In the last year of her life, my Aunt March developed a common ailment that afflicts many werewomen who reach the age of one hundred, a bad case of rheumatism. Though it was mild at first, in time it inflamed her joints and paralyzed her limbs to the point where everyday activities became exceedingly difficult. Eventually, she could hardly change from human to Lupine form, crack open a deer skull without assistance, or climb the slopes of Fairhaven Hill for our pack's midnight rites honoring Mother Luna. But the hardest blow came when her once dignified stride slowed to a creeping hobble, turning her morning stroll into an excruciating ordeal.

A reasonable werewoman would have stopped going out walking on those cold New England mornings, especially after they had been repeatedly advised against it by the local herbalist. A sensible werewoman wouldn't have needed to be told. Yet, neither reason nor sense stood in the way of Aunt March's decision to keep going out, exactly as she had done for decades. Her walks began at precisely ten o'clock each morning and ended at half-past eleven, yielding an hour and a half of horrendous torture. Reason shivered alongside Aunt March's stiff and trembling limbs. Sense clenched her jaws, bared her teeth, and suffered the stroll regardless.

Those of us who tended to her in those last months could see how hard it was for her to take those walks, grimacing as she went; her cane held firmly through each spasming step. Trying to prevent her from going was futile, of course. One might as well have attempted to hold back the tide or stop the changing of the seasons, for she ignored every argument and shouted down every protest until we simply gave in.

On occasion, a morning visitor would come to pay their respects, arriving just in time to see Aunt March struggling towards the front door. With ill-advised chivalry, the visitor might try to talk her into staying in, offering the excuse that it looked like rain. Really, they would say, in light, casual tones that fooled no one, she ought to stay in and avoid the downpour. Much better to sit by the fire and have a nice cup of hot *izgarva* tea than be drenched!

Her reaction to this unsolicited advice was always the same. First, she would treat the visitor to a long, incredulous stare, then she would give a sharp snort of derision, and finally she would unleash a brief, but fiery lecture. Ah, I still recall every sardonic word...

"In the name of Mother Luna's luminous grace," Aunt March would say, "am I expected to cower inside forever because of bad weather? Just think how different the history of our species might have been if we did as you suggest. Ozrit might never have led his followers across the burning wastes on account of the ash and smoke. Gorgristram and his pack might have declined General Washington's plea to fight the British at Yorktown on account of a little hurricane. And instead of leading the Wolf Marines to victory against Napoleon II's legions at St. Brelade back in '38, my own darling mate might have said, 'Thank you, Commander Laurence, sir for your order, but no. Not in the midst of this inconvenient hailstorm...'

"*Feh sagahr*!" she would exclaim. "I didn't live this long to just lurk in the parlor and fret about the weather. You young folks! So timid these days…" And with that, she'd sniff imperiously and go off to take her stroll in the garden – very slowly perhaps, with a gait that seemed brittle and stiff, but with tremendous pride and dignity.

Back then, I attributed my aunt's tirades and rigid habits to her prickly, contrary nature. Forty years later, I've started to think it might have been something more. Now I see that once she'd chosen something – a cloak, a companion, or a path – she stuck with it, no matter what, all the way to the end. As irritating as my diminutive relation could be, as infuriating as she was, I could never deny that she had a powerful will and a fierce sense of determination, even if it made her seem like an unbearable grump.

However one chooses to describe it, I think that the force that kept old Aunt March going for one hundred tumultuous years has a deep, elemental quality. Some version of it has manifested itself in wolf-men and werewomen since Mother Luna first touched us with her light and bestowed the Gift upon us, long, long ago. The secret to our survival across the eons might be the same impulse that drove Aunt March out into the garden every single day, despite her pain.

The sound of my aunt's cane stamping slowly along on the garden path had a ring to it, an obstinate defiance that also resounds in our legends and lore. From the Lupine protagonist who confronts an invincible foe, to the lost cub who braves the unknown for the sake of love, to the lone wolf-girl who overcomes sadistic monsters in a dark and terrible place, that unyielding quality can be found on each page of this volume – and particularly in one of my favorite tales, a story known as *Little Red Raging Hood.*

Some human readers might be confused by this. Some of you are probably frowning, furrowing your brows, and saying to yourselves, "That's wrong, it's 'Little Red *Riding* Hood,' the one with the wolf and grandma. I know it well."

Yes, I'm sure you think you do know that story. How could you not? It feels so old, as if somewhere, on a sooty cave wall there are little figures in red-hooded cloaks crudely daubed next to sketches of wooly rhinoceri and giant sloths. Well, I'm sorry to report, human reader, that the version of the story you believe you know is wrong. Not in a subtle or minor way either, but absolutely, totally incorrect in every way that matters.

Here are the facts. The "Little Red Riding Hood" that you are familiar with is an insipid cliché. Humans everywhere, including you, dear *ohusim*, have fooled yourselves into believing that your story is the original. I assure you, it is not. The version you have been told is revised, heavily modified for human tastes and preferences to include a helpless human girl, a brave human hero, and a bloodthirsty, wolfish villain who meets a deservedly gruesome fate. It's a very simple tale, told so often that you've never bothered to wonder how it came to be—or who told it in the first place.

When I was contacted by the publishers and asked to lead the creation of a series that would bring the "exotic lore of the wolf-men to a human audience," I agreed to do so under a specific set of conditions:

First, I would include several unabridged essays and set the record straight about matters of importance, including the truth about *Little Red Raging Hood*. They agreed.

Second, while I would be happy to curate and polish the

collection, under no circumstance would I be responsible for translating it into English. While it is true that in my early years I penned more than a few retellings of Lupine tales for a human audience, the stories included here are different. Many of the stories destined for this collection were first told to me by my father in the ancient language of our species. That memory is so dear to me, I could not permit myself to write them in English. Such translations are actually quite hard to do well, particularly when one has such strong ties to the material. The harsh, decorative patois that we *anutsim* speak is very different from the brisk efficiency of American English.

I informed the publisher they'd need not only a good translator, but an exceptional one – and that I would need to approve their work before it went to print. They agreed, though I sincerely doubted that they would find anyone qualified. Despite my doubts, a worthy candidate was found: a historian and linguist by the name of Mr. J.H. Archibald.

My misgivings were many, but I must admit that Mr. Archibald has done an excellent job in the end. His translations of *Little Red Raging Hood* and the other stories in this collection are definitely worth the ink with which they are printed, and a great deal more besides. He may not be a pleasant man to work with; on the contrary, the process of producing this first volume with him made my head ache and my blood boil with rage. However, the same qualities which make him such a difficult personality, from his pedantic and infuriating obsessiveness to his plodding insistence on attending to every little detail, have produced something remarkable.

I sincerely hope that you, dear reader, may experience even a little of the truth, the pleasure, and the wisdom that these stories have given me over the decades. It took a long while to complete this little book and there were many times when I thought it would have been far easier to quit, to come in out of the proverbial rain and find a warm spot by the fire.

I couldn't though, for each time I closed my eyes, the slow tap of a cane on wet ground would haunt my dreams and the memory of a sharp, critical voice would rise in my mind. And so it went, word by word, line by line, page by page; I kept going in response to that unforgiving ancestral urge.

Now that it is done, I'm amazed to find how pleased I am with the result. Even the most prickly, unbearable grump might approve...

Even Aunt March.

   -J.M.

Translator's Note

Lupines, sometimes referred to more colloquially as wolf-men, are most often praised for their physical attributes, their contributions to music, their service in our nation's military, or their entrepreneurial achievements in business and industry. They are not usually associated with any works of literature other than their three holy scriptures: the Litany, the Edict, and the Analects. Yet those three works may be far older than anything produced by humanity. First as clay tablets, then as vellum scrolls, and finally as books, evidence from the famous Erta Aleh Expedition (1882) suggests that they have been preserved for nearly 15,000 years, well before humankind had built the first crude cities or determined the rudiments of agriculture.

The collapse of the ancient Lupine Dominion in ~15,000 BCE nearly destroyed all traces of their remarkable civilization, including these three sacred books. Thankfully, the nearly superstitious habits of their species preserved these writings throughout the ages, right to the present day.

The topic of this publication, however, is not the religious writings of the Lupines, but another set of works. This volume reveals Lupine story-telling traditions, myths, tall-tales, and fables. Although these works are unknown outside of a small group of academic experts, they constitute what we humans collectively call "folklore."

I first became aware of Lupine folklore during my work as a consultant surveyor on the Cross-Species National Census (1902-1904). During this time, when I went den-to-den to collect statistics on pack demographics and pedigrees, I began to hear many of these folktales, few of which had been translated or printed in any human language, including English. This collection, therefore, represents the first systematic effort by a qualified translator to record and organize these stories for publication.

In this volume, Miss Josdarama March has thoughtfully selected several pieces from her pack's private library for the inaugural volume; the first of a series of twenty-four that will be issued over the next three years by Octavius & Sons, Ltd.

Some of the stories in the collection are incredibly old. The oldest may have been first told in ancient times under dark, star-strewn skies by wolf-men wearing bronze armor whilst sharpening their ceremonial blades. Entries such as *Miracle of the Mice* and *The Story of Aphoph* are among the oldest and may predate human civilization by several thousand years. Other stories in this book are much newer, dating only as far back as the 16th or 17th century. A perfect example of these more modern fables is *Little Red Raging Hood*. The origins of that particular story are obscure, but it may parallel Lupine historical accounts of a mysterious "Valley of the Wolves," a secret society of Lupines that were believed to have retreated to alpine strongholds throughout Europe in escape of human pursuit. Whether these hidden strongholds are factual or merely a work of fiction is impossible to say, as no actual evidence of such secret valleys has ever been found.

In addition to folklore, this book contains several brief essays and historical accounts that provide context for the stories themselves. Discerning readers will appreciate how inventive Lupine minds have transformed historical facts into animated belief systems. Truly, the Lupine imagination is nearly as clever as any human flight of fancy. Those who doubt it need look no further than *The Merchant & The Monster* which appears to be an 18th century European fable. Provided by Miss March, it is obviously a work of pure fantasy loosely constructed from a hodge-podge of semi-historical accounts.

One might wonder why the wolf-men created these stories, whether they served some purpose that paralleled our own human tendency to pretend, invent, and embellish. There are many perspectives on this question, but I believe it was best summarized by the late Professor L. Ovell-Gorham:

> *It should come as no surprise that the wolf-men have faerie-tales and bedtime stories. Why shouldn't they? Even a werewolf needs her offspring to behave, to go to bed, and to eat their dinner promptly before it gets cold—or runs away...*

With that, I will conclude my note. I trust readers will distinguish between carefully researched, factual histories and the highly fanciful, entertaining folktales of Lupine origin.

I wish to thank Miss Josdarama March for her collaboration and the publisher, Mr. Charles Octavius, Sr. for his bold commitment to this remarkable series. I look forward to many more to come.

 -J.H. Archibald, M.Phil., A.B.

The First Litany
& The Last Gift

Translated by J.H. Archibald

Translator's Note: The oldest and longest of the three Lupine sacred texts is the Litany. A sprawling book, encompassing over a thousand chapters; many of the passages in the Litany are meant to be recited in call-and-response fashion between prayer leader and pack.

The first chapter of the Litany describes the creation of the world by Mother Luna, the benevolent, eternal deity that wolf-men worship as supreme and all-knowing.

The translation provided here is taken from the inscriptions recorded at the site of the Erta Aleh Expedition in 1882 and may reflect the original text more accurately than standard versions.

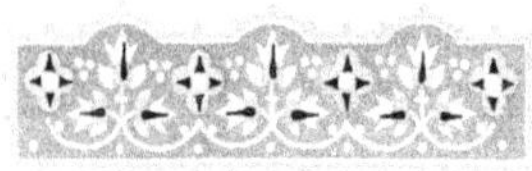

First Book *of the* Litany
Chapter I, Verses I-VII

"The Three Words of Light."

I.   On the night that Mother Luna first rose in the sky, there was nothing above and nothing below. Only the endless black of silent, starless oblivion filled the void.

II.   After a time, Mother Luna spoke the first word that willed all things into existence, *Oda*. Her voice was a ray of pure light, divine and brilliant, and from it the world was formed.

III.   Stone, dust, water, and wind flowed from her first word; life soon followed in all forms and magnitudes, giving rhythm and motion to the land, to the water, and to the air itself. Yet, the first word that Mother Luna had spoken was wanting – the work of creation unfinished – and so she spoke again.

IV.   *Ohusim*, the second word of light; *ohusim* the 'unchanging ones.' With that word, the first humans were willed to rise up from the new clay of the earth. They walked upright and wondered at the vast expanse of the world. They were clever and daring. They created and explored, but when they looked up into the sky, they did not know Mother Luna's face and they could not hear her voice. Thus, the second word she had spoken was wanting, and so she spoke once more.

V.   *Anutsim,* the third word of light; *anutsim* the 'changing
      ones.' With that word, the first wolf-men were willed to rise
      up from the same clay that had given rise to the *ohusim*
      before them. These new creations knew Mother Luna's
      shining face and heard her voice of pure light.

VI.   When the *anutsim* first stood and looked up at Mother
      Luna, they discovered that she had blessed them with the
      Gift, the power of transformation between forms and
      magnitudes. They knew her to be their creator, the speaker
      of the words of light.

VII. When *anutsim* raised their voices to her, howling in her
      praise, she smiled upon them and was pleased, for together
      her words were now complete and perfect.

Foreword to "The Last Gift"

All Lupines I have ever met know the First Litany. Regardless of how devout they might be, no matter the sect or tradition to which they might belong, all of them know the words. Many of them even believe those words and will insist that their faith in the First Litany is strong. They believe it, they declare, with all their heart, from the tops of their pointed ears to the tips of their terrible claws.

But what does that mean? What do these devout wolf-men actually believe with such unbreakable conviction?

Like many religious works, the First Litany is subject to interpretation. While most worshippers agree broadly on certain things, i.e., the general concept of Mother Luna and the fact of our own existence, beyond that there is little consensus and many arguments. For example – is the 'clay' described in the First Litany actual clay or a mystical allegory? Were the three 'words of light' that were spelled out in the text actually audible? How long did all of this creation take? And how could Mother Luna, perfect and supreme, have spoken any word that was 'wanting' or imperfect? How did she get things wrong the first time around and what prompted her to create us, the *anutsim*, her changing, howling children?

The list of questions is as endless as the debates they inspire. Most of those debates are left to religious scholars, devoted Monks of Luna, reverend elders – all those gray and serious wolf-men of purpose and dignity. While the sages nod, ponder, and reflect, the rest of us get on with the task of believing that we were willed from clay and thus formed the perfection that Mother Luna sought.

Our beliefs place humans at a great disadvantage because, while most humans don't believe in Mother Luna, they do believe in themselves – very much so. We can tell them our Lupine stories, but they can only hear through human ears, with human expectations of what our "werewolf scriptures" must contain. To them, there must be conflict and perhaps terror; characters and tragedy; triumph and a moral. Humans have limited patience for words of pure light and disembodied will, even when that will takes on a form (or two) later on. No, when a well-meaning *ohusim* asks us what we Lupines *really* believe, they do not want to hear about metaphysical clay and philosophical uncertainty. They want to hear the *actual* story of how Lupines first came to be in the world. Do we Lupines really want to tell it?

The story that you are about to read appears nowhere in the Litany, nor the Edict, and certainly not in the Analects. It is a story with no actual title, and one that few Lupines would ever admit to ever having heard, yet we have, each of us, heard one version or another of this tale, but we all most certainly will deny it, each of us. Particularly werewomen.

Werewomen will adamantly insist they have never been told any story like this, especially not by their mother, nor their aunt, nor some other female relation on a night that may have been very dark and windy, when they might have been very scared and alone. None of them ever promised to pass this story on to another nor swore an oath on their bloodline that they would not leave this world before this story had been told again.

I hereby discharge that non-existent oath, but I take some risks putting it into print. Much about the tale that I will share could be regarded as blasphemous, as contradicting the First Litany as there is no mention of oblivion, clay, or other sundry details. Such discrepancies might make some readers very angry, but I am delighted to be unqualified on such matters. Some kinds of shouting are best left to those reverend wolf-men who are qualified to shout, or at least qualified to write long, angry, tedious letters. I've warned the publisher to expect them.

I still choose to take the risk and put this story into print, for the times demand it. There is something coming, something that I have not felt since I was young, when the foundations of the world were shaken by the threat of war. All the newspaper headlines bear ill tidings now and all the aetheric transmissions from Europe and the Antipodes crackle with ominous warnings. Every time I close my eyes, I can feel the clouds rolling in and the stars fading overhead. These are troubling days, dark days, so I take the risk and commit this to print because somewhere, someone feels lost and alone.

We all need something to believe in, no matter our age, sex, or species. Even if we don't agree what it is, where it comes from, or what it means, we need to know that there is something more than predation and terror; that there is something more waiting for us than a return to oblivion.

Let there be more than just silence and darkness. Let there be a voice. And let there be light.

-J.M.

The Last Gift

Long ago, before the Dominion of ancient times, before the Splintering, before the migration into the Sacred West, before the Imperii Luporum, before any *anutsim* existed anywhere in the world, a human woman wandered alone in the night. Lost and outcast, beaten and exhausted, her life was in terrible danger.

Mere hours before, at twilight, she had been exiled from her clan, having been declared a 'demon-witch' by the holy man of her tribe. There were many reasons why the holy man might have said such things about the human woman. Maybe it was because she didn't look respectfully at the ground when he spoke, or maybe she mumbled, or became distracted during the ceremonies that he led. But the main reason, she thought, was because she hadn't let him 'cleanse' her of evil spirits on the night before her wedding as their clan traditions required. When he tried to lead her away for the rite, she kicked him most disrespectfully, knocked him down, and ran off to hide.

She hid the entire night, hoping her betrothed would find her and understand why she had run, but he did not come to protect her. Instead, she was found the next morning and dragged in front of the council who were to decide her fate. The holy man gave his best performance, shouting and growing red-faced, spittle sprayed from his cracked lips. He bellowed that she was a witch who had caused the river to go dry; that she had scared away all the game by mumbling curses; that a demon in her eyes made him weak and knocked him down when he tried to cleanse her.

The council deliberated the matter and, though her brothers argued in her favor, others sided with the holy man. The worst was yet to come. The man with whom she was betrothed, her sworn husband-to-be, came forward to accuse her of being confined with another man's child. He didn't look at her when he spoke, but glared at the holy man who leered back at him in a manner that wasn't very holy.

Her brothers, ashamed and upset, asked her if this was true, if she was really with child. They shook her when she refused to answer. When they demanded to learn the father of the child in her belly, she bit her lip and looked away.

The council made up their mind very quickly after that. At sunset, her brothers held her firm while her betrothed struck her many times. None of them wanted to do it, she knew, but the holy man's power was great. The clan would have killed them all if they didn't obey. The holy man nodded while the crowd chanted in low, seething murmurs that sounded like the bubbles from a hot cauldron. She felt the child inside her belly go still and cold as the beating continued, and she no longer had the strength to hold back her tears.

When she finally broke, the holy man clapped his hands together once, as if nothing unusual had occurred, as if it were any other night when the time had come to put out the fire and go to sleep. As the night watch took their places near the perimeter, she was dragged to the edge of the camp, and told she was no longer part of the clan. The holy man took a looming step toward her and, when she stumbled in fear, he laughed and laughed, his croaking voice rising and falling. Unsteadily, she groped her way into the deepening twilight.

As night fell, the heat of the day fell away and the wind increased. Heavy clouds rolled in from the north to blot out the stars. It became so dark that she could see only a few feet in front of her. At first, she thought she would go to a little patch of woodland and hide in a tall tree until morning. There was no sound but the chirp of insects and the rustle of little creatures in the grass, but as she approached, she sensed something large in the undergrowth. It made no noise at all, but followed her silently on padded paws. A predator stalked her, drawn to the blood from her wounds. It crept closer, waiting to pounce, to kill, to strip every bit of lean flesh from her bones.

Uncertain and afraid, she picked up a rock and backed away slowly. She managed to find her way to the edge of the dry riverbed. It was open ground, at least, and she was good at throwing rocks. Much faster and more accurate than her brothers, she could hit any target right between the eyes. She wouldn't be able to kill a big predator, but maybe she'd delay it for a little while she thought, or at least hurt it before it made a meal of her. She waited, crouching tensely in the cold sand, gripping her rock tightly...

She must have nodded off to sleep, for she was startled awake by a bright light from somewhere overhead. Looking up in wonder, she heard a voice speaking to her – but not in the usual way. This voice made no sound that her ears could perceive, and yet somehow she heard it clearly.

You have suffered, it said. *You have been hurt and abandoned by those who should have protected you. Now you are alone in the darkness.*

She did not respond, but she squinted at the light to see if she could figure out what it was. More words soon followed.

You are without weapons, without warmth, without food, and you are being hunted by a very dangerous animal. Soon, you will die.

Though the woman wished it were not so, she knew the voice was speaking the truth.

If you wish to live, there are gifts that will help you. You may have them, if you are willing to accept them and the burdens they might bring. Do you accept them?

The pain made it hard to concentrate, but the woman nodded. She was willing to take whatever gifts she could get, burdens and all, if they might help her to live through the night. The light overhead grew brighter as the voice spoke again.

So it shall be. The first gift is healing. Your body and the bodies of your offspring will heal quickly. You will be immune to sickness, impervious to injury. This is your first gift.

Suddenly, all the bruises and pains on the woman's body started fading, the fractures in her bone knitted themselves together, and the sharp ache in her belly disappeared. By the time the voice spoke again, every cut, scrape, and scar she had ever suffered was gone, as if they'd never happened.

The next gift is one of strength. You shall be stronger, faster even than the creature which hunts you now. You will have increased stamina and will outlast any who strike against you. Your eyes, ears and nose will awaken to the world surrounding you. You will sense everything with tremendous clarity. This is your second gift.

The woman's vision flared, painfully at first. She shut her eyes for a minute before opening them slowly and carefully. When she did, everything she saw in the nighttime landscape, every rock, every thorn, every dry stalk of grass was clear and bright. Her ears picked up every little sound with crispness and clarity. Her nose was flooded by a swirl of scents from the air, more complex and fascinating than she had ever experienced. As she raised her head to catch the wind and inhale the intoxicating tapestry of sight, sound, and smell, the voice spoke again.

Now for the third gift, the greatest of all: Transformation. Your body will be yours to change because you will have a second form, one that is truer to your heart. You will never be cold in this new form, you will never be without the means to hunt – and you will always have the power to defend yourself from the things that hunt you in turn.

The clouds overhead parted now, revealing a brilliant full moon, brighter and more intense than any she had ever imagined. A tremor passed through her and she convulsed with pain, excruciating, at first, but bearable as it progressed. Her skin burned, her bones writhed, everything moved and twisted and grew. When it was over, she looked down to find that she was much taller than before. Her body had grown a pelt of perfect gray fur everywhere, and her fingers were tipped with long talons, sharper and harder than the flints she had once used to scrape skins and cut meat from carcasses. A long, elegant tail swept out behind her, giving her balance and poise. What was she now, she wondered? She touched her face and was surprised to find a long nose and a pair of powerful jaws filled with sharp, white teeth. Maybe she was a demon, just like the holy man had said. Was she immortal?

You are not a demon nor are you immortal, the voice said, reading her thoughts. *You are alive and like all living things, you will die someday. You can be killed and you can succumb to your burdens. Hear them now, the burdens that come with your gifts....*

A cloud passed across the brilliant moon and despite the heat from her new body, the werewoman shivered.

The gift of healing also comes with the burden of vulnerability. You will be immune to all diseases and poisons except one: silver. Beware this moonlight-metal, the one called silver. It robs you of your gifts and brings agonizing death. Beware it and know you are vulnerable.

And the werewoman nodded in acknowledgement, though she didn't really understand, and the voice went on to describe the second burden.

With strength comes desire and hunger. All prey, all flesh may be yours for the taking. In time you will feel the urge to kill for the sake of killing. You will wish to eat and eat and eat, just for the sake of eating. If you do so, in time you will become no more than a hungry stomach, a gaping mouth driven by mindless desire – a bottomless, insatiable Maw.

The young werewoman, after a lifetime of struggling and foraging for survival, could not imagine the concept of gluttony, but she nodded anyway. Satisfied, the voice told her, at last, of the final burden.

Transformation, the greatest of your gifts comes with the heaviest burden: blood-rage. When you confront a foe in battle, your blood-rage will rise up. It will make you fierce and unstoppable, powerful beyond imagining. It will bring you the victories you seek, and with it you will triumph over all adversaries. But left unchecked, it will also make you blind to suffering, a cruel and merciless force of destruction. It will turn you into a tool of oblivion and you will bring pain and death to everything you love.

This time, the young woman understood enough of what the voice said to be horrified. She had a premonition of dread and an image of her whole clan, including her brothers and her mother flailing in pain and screaming for mercy. Their frail human skin had been flayed from their bodies and they had been placed in the branches of a gigantic tree. They clung there, crying and whimpering while underneath the tree, dark forms drooled and waited for them to fall to the ground like ripe fruit. One by one they fell, and when they hit the ground, they were caught and torn to pieces in a hellish cacophony of tearing gristle, snapping bones, and savage snarls...

No, she begged, shaking all over. Silently, she pleaded with the voice, asking to be spared that burden. How could she rid herself of it? How could she hide from it, this terrible blood-rage?

You cannot avoid it, nor should you try to. You will need it, despite the danger it carries. There is no hiding from it, for it lives in your blood and it flows through your bloodline. Soon it will pass to your son – and your daughter!

Something stirred inside her and she froze in amazement. Could it be? She looked back up at the moon and tilted her head questioningly.

Yes, it is true. Soon you will have two cubs. They are your bloodline, your final gift, and your final burden. You must be their light and a voice in the darkness for them to look up to. See that they learn to master all the burdens you pass on to them, to give solace and sanctuary to those in need, and to take no more than they truly require. As long as they do so, your bloodline will flourish from this place and time, and across the generations.

The woman, now a werewoman, dropped to all fours and bowed her head in thanks. She silently averted her eyes in supplication and groveled, the same way she had been taught to grovel before the holy man and his gods, but the voice stopped her.

Do not look away, it said, *but meet my gaze as one mother to another. Sing, be happy, and know what it means to be unbowed by fear. Let your voice soar, all the way to the sky, and beyond...*

Long jaws parted, the newly-sharp nose pointed at the silvery circle of moonlight overhead, and from the ache deep within her belly there emerged the first howl of the *anutsim,* the first howl that ever echoed across the world. The predator in the bushes fled in panic at the sound and far away, the men of the clan woke from their slumber in a cold, guilty sweat. Across the endless stretches of grassland, forest, mountain and desert, the sound carried, mournful yet joyous.

Many seasons later, when the wandering clan returned to the region, two hunters followed a herd of antelope that took them much farther than they'd intended to go. They lost the trail on a high, rocky outcrop at sunset and were forced to turn around and head back. They had only made it halfway when a rough growl froze them in their tracks. Four sets of glowing, feline eyes appeared in the lengthening shadows, floating above four long, saber-toothed grins.

The brothers stood back-to-back and prepared to defend themselves, waiting for a violent, hungry death...

But it never came. Something else moved in the rocks, and they caught glimpses of long, leonine bodies fleeing, ears flattened against their skulls and tails tucked between their legs. Then, the two brothers spotted a tall silhouette in the last light. It made a gesture that looked familiar, though the hand that waved to them was not precisely human. A flash of green-blue eyes looked hauntingly like the eyes of their long-dead sister, as did two smaller sets of nearly identical eyes that hovered nearby for a moment, then disappeared.

When the brothers returned the next day to investigate further, they found three sets of prints that led directly into the mysterious plateaus that rose up to the east. They followed the trail for a while, but before they could get too far, a piercing howl stopped them in their tracks. It was not the threatening call of a predator on the hunt nor was it a lonesome, animal cry. Though neither of the brothers could explain how they knew, both were certain that it was a farewell to them, a final expression of love to them both – and a warning never to return.

Immediately, they ran back to camp to tell the holy man all that they had seen and heard. The holy man's reaction was extraordinary, their words sending him into a panic. Clutching at his chest and gasping for breath, he ordered the clan to break camp, to leave at once and to put as much distance as they could between themselves and the haunted plateaus. Weakened by the pains in his chest, the holy man collapsed, and was carried away on a makeshift litter as the terrified clan fled in haste. He died at sunset, his face frozen in a fearful stare, fixed on a beautiful eastern moonrise.

In the centuries that followed, all the clans of humans avoided the forbidden lands. Legends spread far and wide of a powerful kingdom that arose on those high plateaus, built around a fantastic walled City. It was an empire of shape-changing wolf-men, stronger than gods and fiercer than demons.At each full moon, when the wind blew down from those cloud-wreathed heights, a chorus of howls could be heard. Travelers who dared to go as far as the sandy banks of a dry riverbed would whisper about the eastern horizon, how it was filled with constellations of glowing eyes, all burning with a fiery blue-green light.

For thousands of years, under a brilliant moon, uncounted legions turned upwards to face the sky to give thanks for the blessings and burdens that ran in their bloodlines, from the First to the Last.

Translated by J.H. Archibald

Translator's Note: The Western Tracts is a collection of parables and tales from the ancient time when Lupine packs were forced to flee their ancestral homeland. For the convenience of those readers who are not already experts in Lupine history, here is a very abbreviated background summary –

After the bloodthirsty tyrant Apollyon is defeated in battle by the noble prince Ozrit, a sect of wicked sorcerer-priests known as the *fakur* summon a terrible and spiteful curse from beyond the stars. A storm of 'living darkness' smites the fabled City of the wolf-men, destroying it and blighting the lands beyond for many leagues.

Diminished and scattered, the packs look to the wisdom and leadership of Ozrit to lead them through the wilderness. Although Ozrit has lost Ullwolbe, one of his two companions, he is supported by the warrior-monk Pradon. Great hardship marks their journey each step of their way from the ruins of the Dominion and into the mysterious and sacred West.

While it may be tempting to tease out portions of the Western Tracts and align them with actual events and evidence, it is necessary to refrain from such amateurish historiography. For example, the destruction of the Lupine Dominion has been attributed to the actions of the mysterious group known only as 'the Fakur,' but there is no proof that they actually existed. Oral histories and material objects suggest that the Fakur were neither a true cult, nor an active subculture in early Lupine society. It is most likely that they never existed.

My own research suggests that these supposed sorcerers were merely allegorical, a metaphysical explanation for natural disasters, such as earthquakes and tidal waves. Having seen the physical evidence at the Erta Aleh site – an area well known to be volcanically active – I can personally attest that this is by far the most reasonable explanation. I shall allow the text to speak for itself.

Four stories from the Western Tracts are featured here:

*   *The Blade & The Staff*
*   *The Miracle of the Mice*
*   *The Tale of Aphōph*
*   *At the Gates of the Western City*

The
Blade
And The
Staff

I. On the second day after the Battle of Aldromar, darkness lay upon the land. The sun did not rise, the stars did not shine in the heavens, and Mother Luna's light did not pierce the veil of smoke and dust that engulfed the sky from one horizon to another.

II. The last living *anutsim* packs, the survivors of war and cataclysm, sheltered in a narrow canyon near the shattered walls of the great City, capital of the Lupine Dominion.

III. Ozrit, slayer of the tyrant and champion of Mother Luna, led the sheltering packs in prayer, "Hear our voices now, as you heard our howls in the desert night, grant us your wisdom and guidance and I will give up this tool of war in your name."

IV. He then laid his blessed *ghythrym*, the blade of his ancestors, on the canyon's dusty earth as an offering to Mother Luna in exchange for the packs' safe passage from that place.

V. Next, he took up a plain wooden staff, the same that had once belonged to his friend, Ullwolbe the Scholar. Holding it aloft, he shouted to the heavens: "This alone shall I carry as I lead your cubs through the burning wastes and the lands beyond. No ax, no sword, no weapon forged will I wield as long as I live. I swear this by the grace of Your Loving Light."

VI. The *tava'ri* rose up at this and spoke as one, saying to Ozrit: "O mighty Ozrit, are we not *anutsim,* and are you not our Prince, greatest among us and beloved of Mother Luna? Though our City lies ruined, we have wealth enough yet to adorn and honor you. Do not abandon your ancestral *ghythrym*, but take it and bear it with pride. Take this gorget of gleaming gold, take this scepter crowned with jewels, for these are the ornaments of a Prince – not the discarded wooden staff of a fallen scholar."

VII. "How then," did the *tava'ri* ask him, "shall we tell the Prince from the pauper, the high-born from the low? If you do not carry the weapons and symbols of our Dominion, then it shall truly fall." Ozrit did not answer them, but took up his *ghythrym* one final time and walked to the path that led from their sheltering hollow towards the City.

VIII. A gust of wind, laden with bitter ash, rushed through the canyon carrying the sounds of untold anguish, a choir of infinite lament, and the cruel, triumphant roar of a hungry, unseen Maw.

IX. With a howl, Ozrit flung his ancestral blade, sending it spinning, end over end into the ravenous dark.

X. Soon, the wind ceased, the shadows thinned, and a single ray of light broke through the murky sky, lighting a path into the far West.

XI.   Pointing the wooden staff towards the dim beacon, Ozrit urged the packs to rise and seek their salvation. "There is her beckoning arm, she reaches out for us and offers us solace from oblivion."

XII.   With those words, he led the packs out of the canyon, away from the place where the City had once stood, out into the desolation of their once mighty Dominion. They trembled when they passed over the crest of the hills and saw the hellish glow emanating from the emptiness of the burning wastes beyond.

XIII.   Fierce Pradon, boldest of the warriors among them, uttered a shrill howl of horror. "How has our once beautiful realm been reduced to this nightmare of cinders? Did we not speak the proper words of prayer to Mother Luna every night? Were our temples and altars not ornate enough to satisfy her eternal and heavenly grace?"

XIV.   Ozrit bowed his head in sorrow before replying: "The words from our lips did not match the truth in our hearts. We said the prayers but we did not live them. We proclaimed our devotion to her luminous light, but we were cruel, refusing sanctuary to those in need, willfully blind to the suffering of the wretched. We twisted her rituals to excuse our worst selves.

XV. "Now we are cast out of this Dominion, into the wilderness. There we shall learn, at long last, to care for one another and to honor all her creations; even the *ohusim*, our human cousins, even the weak and the crippled amongst us. When we have finally demonstrated that we truly believe the prayers we speak, that we can treat all her cubs with kindness, then perhaps she will allow us to return."

XVI. And with that, Ozrit stepped out into the smoky darkness, Pradon at his side, and the surviving packs followed.

*Thus began the perilous journey
into the sacred
West.*

The Miracle
of the Mice

*H*unger lit a ravenous fire in the throats of the migrating packs; picking at bones in dry riverbeds, the bellies of their cubs swelled with emptiness.

They came upon a village of *ohusim*, humans with thin bodies toiling to keep the harvest from being consumed by the mice that plagued their fields.

'How can it be fated,' pleaded the pack leaders, all the noble *tava'ri*, 'that we shall go hungry, that our own cubs beg us for food and Mother Luna places this gift in our path? Are we to spare the *ohusim* while we watch our cubs starve and perish?'

And Ozrit spoke unto them: 'Sooner should we eat of our own flesh than to take *ohusim* as prey; Mother Luna has not led us here to provide a feast of depravity but to test our strength. We must seek her will and know it clearly, humbly and without malice, only then may we learn how to live as anutsim are meant to.'

The *tava'ri* bowed their heads and accepted this judgment, though they feared for the survival of their packs. They went off to prowl the barren hills, hoping to discover some meager prey or a little forage that they might stave off hunger for one day more, but they found nothing there but dry and empty watercourses, withered scrub, and lifeless stone.

In the sleepless, starving night-time, while their parents hunted in the hills, the little cubs crept into the grain fields that night, though none could say what drew them there. To their delight and surprise, every inch of ground and each stalk of the grain was laden with mice, thousands upon thousands of them, all fat and plump from devouring the humans' grain harvest.

The cubs swept through the fields, gorging themselves on the rodents that would have eaten the remainder of the humans' grain. Even in their frenzied hunger, they could consume no more than one third of the vermin that swarmed there.

By the time the first rays of dawn appeared in the east, they were all so full, they could hardly drag themselves back to their hidden dens to fall asleep in a daze of contentment and full stomachs.

Upon their return from their fruitless hunting, the *tava'ri* were amazed. All of them waited eagerly for the next sunset, and even the proudest of them could not resist joining their cubs in the fields when darkness fell. Each and every one put aside their pride and fed well upon the bounty, giving praise to Mother Luna for her grace and mercy – and to Ozrit for his faith and wisdom.

The bounty in the fields helped to sustain the packs on their long migration while also saving the lives of the humans who went on, blissfully unaware how Ozrit's judgment had saved their own lives. All they would ever know was that one one autumn night, when the moon hung full and low in the sky, some mysterious force made the plague of mice vanish, leaving no trace behind except for a few bent stalks of grain...

....and one mysterious footprint in the dust, very much like that of a gigantic wolf.

'The Miracle of the Mice' is commemorated every Ozritmas with the ritual consumption of pickled mice. This delightful tradition is enjoyed by young and old alike.

The Legend *of*
Aphōph

Another popular parable from the Western Tracts speaks of Aphōph, a strange insectile being that lurked in the sands, waiting to catch the unwary and drag them back to its nest to nourish its young. In the middle of the Great Migration, several cubs were snatched away in the middle of the night. Only the bravery of Ozrit and his companion, the fearsome and mysterious Pradon saved the cubs from a terrible fate...

As Mother Luna set and the sun rose over the eastern hills, Ozrit and Pradon returned, each carrying a lost cub in their arms, reuniting the litter with their wolf-mother; rescued from the nest, the cubs had been spared the torment of Aphōph's sting and the agony of Aphōph's eggs in their living bodies.

The pack rejoiced and fell to the sands in gratitude, thanking Ozrit and Pradon, praising their bravery, and cursing Aphōph as an evil and wicked thing that should be destroyed; all about them Lupine warriors howled and looked towards the burning wastes where the deadly creature nested.

But rather than unleash their fury on the thing which had nearly claimed two of their own, Ozrit spoke softly but clearly, and his voice passed gently to each member of the pack, turning their wrath to calm and their anger to acceptance. Thus he spoke:

'Would you have the creatures of the forest curse us as evil for hunting to feed our cubs? Would you have the river regard us as wicked for drinking its water to quench our thirst? Aphōph's need for prey is no more evil than the turning of the seasons and no more worthy of your rage than drought, flood, fire, or cold.

'It is the nature of Aphōph to raise offspring, just as we do. We have no cause to fear or hate Aphōph, only to understand it, respect it, and know it has stalked these dunes for longer even than we *anutsim* have roamed the land...'

And So Ozrit Said:

'Strive each day to
be peaceable; in
harmony with all
living things
according to
their own
Truth.'

A·t T·h·e
Gates

o·f T·h·e
Western
City

Translator's Note: The final passages of the Western Tracts, the last book of the Analects, describes the end of the great western migration and the last acts of the *anutsim* survivors as they completed their escape from the blighted lands of the Dominion. The following passages include the famous "Assembly on the Dunes," the handing over of the Ossuary to Pradon, and the last words of Ozrit as he set out across the Endless Sea.

On The Shores of the Endless Sea

I. On the last day of the long migration, on the shores of the Endless Sea, the wolf-men who gathered on the sand were different from the ones that had fled the destruction of the City so long ago. Gone were the decadent trappings, the fine robes, the gleaming jewels. Gone were the scepters and ornaments, the tokens they had once gripped in fear. Most carried no weapons aside from their own teeth and talons.

II. The wolf-men clustered on the shore were far fewer in number than those who had first set out. In the first year, nearly a quarter of them had been lost to disasters, weakened by hunger, and scarred by events.

II. The packs' survivors found themselves looking out at a limitless expanse of ocean, greater than any they had ever seen before. Not even the scouts or the farseers among them could find the opposite shore, no matter how carefully they scanned the horizon. All that could be seen were the peaks and valleys of gray-green waves that disappeared over the edge of the world.

Assembly *on the* Dunes

I. Together, the survivors of migration, misery, and loss stood on the dunes and were stunned by the quiet. No enemy swarmed at their flanks, no brooding evil sought their blood, and for the first time in seven long years, they knew a true feeling of peace.

II. Ozrit clambered up on a high dune to address the assembly and the masses fell to their knees, crouching in the sand to hear his words. They worshiped him, unashamed and with fervor, for the day he had prophesied had finally come to pass. Even the greatest doubters among them found faith there, and every last one of them believed with all their might that he was truly the chosen of Mother Luna. The sound of their faith was louder than the roar of the waves, though no ear could hear it. The light it made was blinding, yet no eye could see it.

III. Together, united, the packs knelt on the sand and waited for their leader, their prophet, the chosen of Mother Luna to speak to them. It felt as though an eternity passed in that deafening silence on the shore, though time itself did not move, as the packs waited in awe for the words that would follow.

The Final Edict

I. When Ozrit finally spoke, his voice shimmered with power, but his words were humble. "Please, do not kneel, my friends. Do not kneel before me," he begged. "I am no more than you are, one among the many, struggling to find the path that Mother Luna has illuminated for us all. Please, rise…" Yet none would rise and none could meet his gaze, for his eyes shone with a heavenly light that was beautiful and terrible beyond measure.

II. Ozrit wept that no one would stand with him, no one would even dare to look at him in that prophetic moment, though he begged and pleaded over and over. Only Pradon, as his *anu'varim*, dared to stand, shake off the clinging sand, and approach him with eyes raised.

III. A little boat lay upon the beach, a fragile thing of skins, stretched over a frail frame of wood. From whence it had come, none knew, but Ozrit found a sigil in the sand, and the lines traced the points of *Othradsim*, the Rejoined. Drawn in the ephemeral sand on that shore, it reflected the constellation above, the shape of the stars that began to reveal themselves in the sky that darkened over the Endless Sea.

IV. As the assembly looked on, no words were exchanged between Ozrit and Pradon for each knew the mind and the heart of the other, better than any could ever know.

V. Ozrit knew then what he must do, as he had always known what would happen when he reached that shore of gorgeous desolation. He spoke once more to the assembly on the dunes, the last Edict he would speak: "Oh, my friends, blood-of-my-blood, we have come at last beyond the greatest of perils. This sign in the sand tells me that this part of our journey, the most perilous part of our migration has ended at last. I have led you to this place, beyond the dangers which plagued us and the evil which sought to destroy us. We will know peace, for a time."

The Offering *of the* Ossuary

I. Pradon, robed and wrapped in the bindings of the Monks of Luna spoke then, saying: "Where shall you lead us next, *Tava'ri* of the Heavens, Bearer of Luna's Light?" for this was the title that the assembly of packs whispered to one another, so complete was their adoration of the one who had led them there.

II. Ozrit smiled at this and refused the honor that Pradon sought to bestow upon him. "My dearest friend, I answer not to those titles. If I am the bearer of Her Loving Light, then so are we all. For I am no greater than the least among you, though I led you here. But I led only for a time, as one who happens to be upwind might lead the hunt, not because I was wiser or holier than any other, but because I was the one who caught the scent."

III. Ozrit stood in the briny wind and bore the great burden of remembering all those who had been lost. As the ocean wind whipped at Pradon's robes and then swept over them both, only the memory of Ullwolbe the Scholar remained distinct. Ozrit took the Ossuary from his belt and handed it to Pradon, who was gripped with anguish at the knowledge of what was to come.

The Gates *of the* Western City

I. Ozrit looked in sorrow at the little boat on the shore, for he did not feel that a vessel so small could bear the weight of the years, the regrets for the heavy deeds he had carried out to help the packs survive. Still, Ozrit stepped into the boat, no less brave on the shores of the Endless Sea than he had been on the banks of the Aldromar.

II. Those who stood upon the shore raised their voices, lamenting as the boat that bore Ozrit was carried away by the waves and the wind. Amongst the clamor and the howls of sorrow, one voice rose above all others – the voice of Pradon, pure and true. Raising the hallowed vessel of the Ossuary, the ashes of their martyred friend Ullwolbe, Pradon said: "When shall we three meet again?"

III. Ozrit's words seemed to come on the waves, carried by the gusts that rose as the night deepened from east to west: "When the world trembles, when sky above and ground below shake and shatter, at the end of all migrations when there is a reckoning of souls–then shall we meet again."

IV. Pradon called back: "Holy Ozrit, *anu'varim*! Name the place and I will carve a path across the cosmos, I shall fell great hordes of our enemies, natural and unnatural, to carry Ullwolbe's ashes and meet you there. Name the place and we will be there on the day when all migrations end."

V. And Ozrit replied: "You will know the place I speak of, and I will raise a mighty city to mark the spot. It will be a home for us to live in, us three, and a sanctuary for all who pass through its gates. Come, meet me at the gates," cried Ozrit, "I have seen the place in my dreams and I see it again now as I look over the horizon. The tops of the towers are visible, even at this distance."

VI. Pradon peered towards the last light of the setting sun, through the wrappings, but even those preternatural eyes failed to spot the towers that Ozrit spoke of. "I do not see it," the Warrior Monk wailed. "Help me to see the City, the Western City at the end of the Endless Sea!"

VII. "You must not look with the eyes of a warrior," Ozrit sang out. "You cannot see them, but with the eyes of a cub, through the innocence that believes in a life which is better than the one we have lived. Oh, I know you will see it, old friend! Someday, you will catch a glimpse of it and then you will never lose sight of it again. It is a shining and golden city, greater even than that which we have lost. The shimmering walls are high, but they do not leave the weak to shiver on the open plain, exposed and cold. The gates are strong, but

they are never closed to those in need. The towers are so
tall, the tops are lost in the clouds, but none are held
captive in their chambers."

VIII. Pradon said something in return, secret words that none
could hear.

IX. Ozrit's reply, the last words he spoke as the moon rose full
and bright over the ocean, was heard clearly by the
Assembly on the Dunes:

"Return and rejoin for a time our cousins, the *ohusim*. Live
in their midst and learn their ways. Obey my Edict, always,
not because I have spoken it, nor because it is the word of
Mother Luna herself, but because it is good and true.
When you come, bring nothing with you except the truth
that you have lived. You warriors amongst you, do not carry
your sharp-edged *ghythrym* to those gates, leave behind the
memories of terrible deeds committed for good causes. You
tava'ri, do not bring your weighty sorrows, leave behind
your heavy thoughts and fears of the decisions made and
not made. You wolf-men, you werewomen all, bring only
yourselves. None shall be turned away."

X. A twinkling light could be seen at the spot where the little
boat sailed over the edge of the world.

XI. "I shall mark a trail for you, one and all, to follow into the
sacred West. The City awaits, and as your numbers grow, so
too shall our City grow. Meet me at the gates! When you
arrive, fearless Pradon, wise Ullwolbe, and I too will be
there to greet you. You will pass through the gates of our
glorious City and join us in peace. In her loving light…"

XII. The remainder of his words were lost in the din of wind,
wave, and faith.

the HIGH-BORN
and
the THING

Translator's Note

Temptation by evil is a common theme in Lupine folklore, particularly in the context of dreams. In every community of wolf-men, from the Southern *anutsim* ascetics of the American swamps to the urbane *sarthandrim* packs of the Provençal city-states, such fables abound. They typically feature an archetypal young Lupine who is confronted by a crafty seducer.

This seducer makes offers of glory while urging our young Lupine hero or heroine to ignore all moral boundaries, defy the holy Edict, and take humans as prey. The conflicted protagonist struggles to overcome the wiles of the wicked dream-foe, but triumphs in the end, only to awaken with the discovery of a physical token of the encounter, often a cryptic scar or battle trophy which confirms the experience was 'more than a dream.'

Miss March has offered up *The High-Born & The Thing*, an Iron Age tale which does follow that ordinary pattern, but only to a point. The ending diverges quite sharply from well-known tropes in a manner that might be disturbing to some readers; those who have an aversion to bloodshed might wish to avoid it. I also must note that the ending offers disturbing allusions to the rise of the Imperii Luporum, though obviously this primitive mythology has no connection to actual historic events. Nevertheless, the protagonist of this story exhibits qualities that are extraordinarily malignant for the usual 'temptation-dream protagonist' archetype.

I am certain that this story is meant only to demonstrate the darker side of crude non-human folktales, so I will not belabor the point. A respected literary werewoman like Miss March will surely have a pithy remark to clarify her choice.

– J.H.A.

Author's Reply

My translator's supposition is entirely correct; I would *never* stoop to suggest anything untoward. For example, it would be very wrong of me to speculate that the shadowy, human worship of a wolf-like demigod during the ancient age of the Imperii Luporum has anything to do with this silly tale.

I'm merely a writer of ridiculous fictions with a penchant for 'primitive non-human mythologizing' as Mr. Archibald might put it. I don't suggest anything at all. I just scribble whatever nonsense my werewoman's fancies happen to surface and append it to this crude folklore.

With that, I wish all of you a pleasant read.

And sweet dreams.

– J.M.

ong after the western migration had come to an end, long after Ozrit disappeared over the distant horizon of the Endless Sea, a young werewoman grew from cub to adult. She was a bold Lupine daughter, born to a strong pack that had flourished amongst the early human civilizations that had bloomed in the age of bronze, but only by keeping their Gift a secret. The cunning and skill of the wolf-men, their keen senses, and their ancient knowledge served them well as they dwelled, unseen in their true forms, within the growing cities. Many became great merchants, artisans, musicians, and craftsmen, and as time passed, they grew wealthy and comfortable.

The werewoman grew up in such comfort, under the doting protection of her parents, and had a life of ease and plenty. The eldest and most beautiful daughter, her sisters sometimes made fun of her, calling her 'High-Born' because of her vain, self-important bearing.

"Hark, the High-Born approaches!" they would shout, dancing around her and bowing in a mocking fashion. "Fetch a blood-warm peacock liver for her refreshment! Strew her path with black rose petals, howl her praises to the sky!"

She glowered and snapped at them as they capered about, but she never protested too bitterly for she knew that their words were not entirely in jest.

When she went to the secret gatherings of the Lupine packs, held in hidden places under the light of the full moon, the young werewoman saw the looks that she received. All the wolf-boys stared shyly, turning their heads submissively whenever she stared back. Each of the wolf-mothers in attendance murmured encouragements to their bashful sons, praising the werewoman's beauty and extolling her bloodline. "There, that is the sort of mate I pray to Mother Luna you might have someday!" they whispered in their own offspring's pointed ears. She knew then that she was indeed a beauty without peer, an earthbound star.

Admired and lavished with luxuries and praise in private, the only real burden in the werewoman's life was the necessary pretense of appearing as an ordinary human woman in public. Each time she left her den to go to the market with her sisters or to watch the performances from the women's section in the amphitheater, she kept her shawl pulled low over her face and her eyes cast downward, as was customary. Passersby spared her no more than cursory glances, seeing nothing but a well-off merchant's daughter, beshawled, aloof, and quiet.

So she went through the streets, all but invisible. When humans of high status walked by, be they distinguished patricians or decadently-garbed priests, all the commoners bowed deferentially. The werewoman followed their example, just as she had been taught, but while she always feigned respect, she felt nothing but resentment. One day, as she knelt before a passing princely retinue, a powerful urge came upon her. Unbidden, she was seized with a desire to tear her shawl from her head, to stand boldly among the groveling masses, and to transform while in full view. Yes, right there, surrounded by humans, she trembled with pleasure at the thought of revealing her true form for all to see!

In the privacy of her waking dream, the imagined crowds would fall to the ground before her, forgetting their princes and abandoning their idols in a frenzy of awe, admiration, and fear. The humans in the werewoman's fantasy found her blazing eyes, her rending teeth, and her wicked talons the only objects worthy of worship. Such a thing was impossible of course. No Lupine would ever dare to appear transformed in front of humans, for a solemn covenant had bound all of them to secrecy since ancient times. Still, the thought haunted her. Even after she returned home, she could think of nothing else. Later that evening, just before supper, she summoned the courage to go to her parents and ask them – was it really necessary that they live like this?

"Mother, Father, *gar agatir*," she said, most respectfully. "Why must we *anutsim* hide our true selves from the humans? We bow our heads to the *ohusim* princes and priests in the streets, the strongest of whom I could snap like a twig. Why? What is the point of tiptoeing around the humans and treating them as though they were our betters?"

Her father said nothing at first, for he had just popped a fat, juicy dormouse into his jaws and was busy crunching it up, bones and all, but her mother wasted no time in speaking her mind. "The answer is obvious, eldest daughter," she retorted. "This has been our way ever since we escaped the destruction of the Dominion. It is Mother Luna's will, praise Her Loving Light!"

"Yes, praise Her Loving Light," echoed the younger werewoman. "But is it really her will? I do not doubt that this charade served some purpose back in ancient times, back when we were few in number and weakened by war and migration, but it has outlived its usefulness. How can Mother Luna still want this for us? We are stronger now, more numerous, more confident."

"This is a tiresome subject," her mother said, dismissively. "I don't wish to discuss it further." But that did not stop the young werewoman from continuing.

"We shouldn't hide what we are," she declared. "We should howl it proudly and claim our rightful place here! Can't you see that?

Or are you just too blind and too old to understand?”

“Ungrateful whelp!” her mother snarled through teeth that were growing long and sharp with fury. It might have gone very badly for the impertinent young werewoman then, but her father reluctantly paused his evening snack and intervened. He spoke in tones of kind, fatherly indulgence, only slightly muffled by the wriggling dormouse disappearing down his throat.

“My sweet little bloodthorn,” he chuckled at his eldest cub, using his favorite nickname for her. “So sharp you are, so deep you cut! It is natural that you might have questions, and it is good to be curious, but take care not to speak disrespectfully to your mother.” He patted his mate’s arm, now covered in bristling fur and tried to soothe her while doing his best to address his daughter’s questions.

“Listen to me, carefully, my dear. This life we have is a good one. Look about you, what do you see?” He waved his free paw at the well-appointed chamber while he plucked another wriggling treat out of the chalice by his side. “Silken tapestries on our walls, golden ornaments on our bodies, sweet honey and freshly killed game in our larders, and far more to be had, should we desire it. No, we do not need to lead, my daughter, merely to live. Here, have a dormouse, they’re quite delicious tonight.”

“Enough of this,” interrupted her mother, glaring at her mate with a look that said she approved neither of his indulgent attitude, nor his dormouse addiction. “Clearly, the time has come to find you a mate so you can get on with having cubs of your own and continuing our bloodline instead of asking rude questions. Who do you think you are, a queen? A goddess? Get out of my sight, no supper for you this evening!”

Ordered to her chamber, the werewoman spent a hungry evening grumbling and reciting the Litany of the Wolf-Mother by herself before finally falling into a fitful sleep.

That might have been the end of it. Her life might have unfolded as planned, with great comfort, certainty, and boredom. She might have found a worthy mate and borne a litter or two of healthy, squirming cubs, all the while fantasizing how the sight of her true glory could have awed and cowered the weak and silly humans into groveling submission. And perhaps that is how it would have gone, but it didn't. For that very night, the Thing appeared to her in her dreams.

"What are you?" she asked it, as it crouched at the end of her bed.

"Me? I'm just a Thing," it gurgled. "A sort of a spirit, you might say."

"A good spirit?" she asked, doubtfully.

"Oh, definitely a good spirit," it assured her. "A *very* good spirit. See these wings? They don't give these to just anybody. Anyway, I come bearing gifts." And with that, it made a strange gesture and pulled something impossibly smooth, polished, and dark right out of thin air.

"What is that?" she asked. The Thing stroked the smooth surface and smiled.

"It's an enchanted mirror, unlike any other in the world. It shows events that have not yet taken place, reflections of things to come," it crooned. In the mirror's dark, flat rectangle, murky images moved and rippled. As the werewoman watched , they grew clearer and brighter. The Thing's dingy looking wings fluttered with excitement.

"Just look!" it whispered with delight. "See there? Your future..."

The werewoman wanted to tell the Thing to leave her alone, to get out of her dreams, but the image in the mirror was entrancing. She saw herself atop a tall hill while hundreds of thousands of humans did her bidding – all while she was in her glorious wolfish form! Her eyes flashed, she howled, she bared her teeth and they all bowed down. Even stranger than that, some of them offered themselves up to be sacrificed for her consumption... Which was forbidden, above all things, but the sight of them begging her to kill them, to eat their still-warm flesh fascinated her.

She was very unsettled, not by the idea itself, but more by the fact that it didn't shock or disgust her the way she thought it would have. Perhaps she should have told the Thing to go away, to say that she was a good *anutsim*, a wolf-girl who believed in the Litany, the Edict, and the Analects. But when she opened her mouth, all she could bring herself to say was, "Is it real?"

"What?" asked the Thing distractedly. It could hardly tear itself away from the pictures of pleading humans. One of them appeared to be scooping his own eyeballs out of his skull and offering them up like small, bloody *hors d'œuvres*.

"I said, is it real?" she repeated.

"Of course, it's real," said the Thing, giving her a hurt look. "I made it myself! Took me ages. Here, listen to this…" It extended a spindly hand and rapped gently on the mirror. There was a faint metallic 'bong' accompanied by weird harmonics that lingered uncomfortably in the air. "Hear that? That's craftsmanship," the Thing proclaimed proudly. "A lot of love went into it. Well, no," it corrected itself, "not love. I get mixed up. What's the opposite of love? I can never remember. Anyway, yes this mirror is definitely real, thank you very much."

"No, what I mean is, how can I be sure that you are showing me my real future? How do I know you are telling me the truth?"

The Thing laughed, a high, twisted little noise that made shivers run up and down her spine. "Of course I'm telling you the truth."

"What if you're not? What if you're lying?" the werewoman pressed. The dull red glow in the Thing's eyes flared for a moment and the shadows that surrounded it grew momentarily darker.

"Why would I lie to you?" it said. "After all, I'm a messenger from a higher power. I'm not allowed to show you anything that isn't true. Keep watching, you'll see…"

The werewoman lapsed into silence as the images continued to flicker in the mirror. Columns of bronze-clad soldiers marched to war at her command, devoted acolytes brought sacrifices to a temple dedicated to her beauty, and hordes of humans fell to the ground to worship her when she transformed on a high pedestal atop a towering hill.

"It can all be yours," promised the Thing. "Just reach through the mirror and take it. Go ahead."

Eagerly, without hesitating, she started to reach out towards the mirror but drew back at the last moment, fearful and uncertain.

"Why did you stop? Don't you like what you see?" the Thing asked. "Don't you want to show the world what you are and be adored and feared, just as you deserve to be?"

"Yes," she gasped. "Truly. But they say I shouldn't do it. They say I have to hide in my human skin. They'll be angry."

The Thing tilted its lumpish head to one side. "You are worried that 'they' might get angry? Don't listen to 'them,'" it urged her. "What do 'they' know? Listen to yourself. Listen to your blood, your heart. And your stomach. That's who you should listen to. Go on, reach in and take your future."

She started to reach but stopped short once more. "What about eating human flesh? That's a terrible violation of the Edict. It's forbidden, it's wrong..."

"Oh, it is," the Thing nodded emphatically. A little dribble of greenish drool ran down its chin. "It's very, very wrong. But is it wrong if the human is telling you to do it? Is it wrong if you only do it symbolically? What if you don't really eat bite them a little to make them feel better? Who is to say it's wrong then?"

"Yes, all fair points but—you're sure you're really a good spirit sent from the heavens? A messenger from Mother Luna?"

"Sure," said the Thing. "You could say that. Now, enough talk. Reach in there and take your future. Quickly! Before you lose the chance..."

This time, the werewoman didn't reach towards the mirror. She looked closely at the Thing for the first time, taking in the ash-colored skin, the bulging, pupil-less eyes, and the pathetic, dirty-gray wings sprouting from its back. She frowned and the Thing shifted uncomfortably.

"Wait a moment," she said. "If this is my future and it is going to happen anyway, why do I need to reach into your mirror?"

"It's complicated," said the Thing. "Metaphysics, dimensional stuff, you know? Hard to explain. Hurry up, though, I can't lurk here all night. Don't you want that future? Get in there and grab it!"

"No," said the werewoman. "I don't think so."

The Thing looked very upset. Its wings twitched like dying butterflies and it started to speak again, arguing that she was going to miss out on a marvelous future, but the werewoman interrupted him almost immediately.

"Either you're lying to me and this isn't my future, or you're telling the truth and it is," she said, firmly. "In which case, I don't need to reach into your mirror to get it. It's fate, it will happen regardless." She drew herself up on the other end of her bed, crouching on her haunches. "So why are you so eager for me to reach into that mirror? Is this some sort of a trick?"

"Listen, you're getting all worked up about nothing," the Thing insisted. "Do you think that I'd try to trick someone as brilliant as you? Steal your soul something? Maybe doom you to an eternity of suffering in the lightless depths of the Maw?"

"Steal my soul?" she repeated, growing more alarmed. In the dream, she felt the same tension building inside her that preceded a transformation. Her talons slid out and cut long slashes in the soft blankets and cushions of her bedding. "What do you mean by 'the Maw?'"

"Nothing, sorry, I was thinking of someone else," the Thing croaked nervously. "You women, sorry, werewomen. Always taking things out of context, ha ha. I didn't mean to upset you." The werewoman crept closer to the Thing, but she didn't reach for the mirror. Tremors ran all through her body as she began to transform. Her Lupine form was much larger and heavier than her human form and her dream-bed groaned alarmingly under the increased mass. The growl that came out of her throat was so low and harsh, it made the mirror vibrate and the images on its surface swirled and faded away.

"Hey," said the Thing, inching backwards until it bumped into the wall. "I'm a good spirit, remember? And this is just a dream. So whatever you might be thinking, you'll never be able to hurt me and you certainly can't kill me. I don't even feel pain. So let's just both calm down and take a deep brea-"

It turned out that the Thing was entirely wrong. Before she killed it, she proved that it could most definitely feel pain. Even in a dream.

An hour before dawn the next day, the werewoman's younger sisters went to her bedchamber to rouse her and invite her to join them for breakfast.

"Get up, High-Born, get up!" they yipped through the door, in the half-teasing, half-loving tone that only siblings can achieve. "Quit lazing about in royal slumber, we are going to hunt for rabbits in the olive groves. Get up!"

When they finally went inside to drag her out, they were confused, then terrified by what they saw. Their mother and father came running when they heard the shouting, demanding to know what was going on, stopping short as soon as they stepped into the chaotic mess of what had once been an expensively decorated room. The bed frame had been smashed to splinters and every single blanket and cushion had been ripped to shreds. The tapestries on the walls were ruined, stained with a dark, oily substance that, on close inspection, proved to be blood. It wasn't Lupine blood, or deer, boar, goat, sheep, cow or pig – nor was it human, and her parents exchanged relieved looks as they each confirmed it separately. In fact, no one could remember having smelled any blood of any sort quite like it before. But it was blood just the same and therefore alarming under the circumstances.

It was obvious that there had been a fight of some kind in the room and that something had been killed. Bloody paw prints and vicious claw marks on every surface told the story of a struggle that had been brief but violent, leaving the floor, walls, and a good part of the ceiling scored and streaked with red-black stains. In addition to the bed, the chair that no one ever sat in, the loom that her parents could never get their eldest daughter to use, and the stove that kept the chill away in the winter were all damaged beyond repair. The only article of furniture that was left intact was the heavy oak chest where extra blankets, cloaks, and the toys that the young werewoman had outgrown were stored. No one wanted to open it, but after an anxious minute, her mother steeled herself and lifted the lid cautiously. After a quick glimpse, she slammed it shut and ordered everyone out except her husband.

In the silence of the empty room, the two of them opened the chest up again to look at a tattered pair of gray, pathetic-looking wings that had been violently torn out at the root. The feathers were starting to crumble to dust and they stank of something they couldn't identify, sulfur-tainted and sweetly putrid. Unable to stand it any longer, they closed the chest back up and quietly carried it out of the room. Later on, they burned the whole thing in a deserted field. As the flames consumed the chest and its contents, they recited the Litany of the Rising Smoke, the traditional words that wolf-men spoke at a funeral after the pyre had been lit.

A little later after that, when the servants came in to sweep up the wreckage and remove all traces of the strange oily blood, they discovered that the bedroom window was open. What they did not know is that someone had jumped from it a few hours earlier and had slunk off silently. The trail they left behind led through the sleeping town, all the way down into the snug little harbor where a squadron of triremes loaded with settlers and supplies for the new colonies across the sea had set sail at daybreak. A few weeks later, a boat washed up in a secluded cove, hundreds of miles north of its intended destination. The captain of this unfortunate vessel would have been infuriated had he seen the state of his ship, for her oars were not in the water and no one was rowing, all the sails hung slackly on the masts while the lines flapped loose, and the ship's prow swayed erratically as the tide pushed it gradually towards the shore.

Fortunately, the captain wasn't able to see this awful sight, but even if he could have, he wouldn't have been able to berate and discipline his crew, for all of them, from the first helmsman to the last indentured oarsman was lying dead in the hold. Throats torn and bellies ripped open, they all served as ballast while the ship they had once served on wedged itself on the beach.

A little while later, a lone figure and the only surviving passenger leapt from the deck down onto the sand. It wore a hooded robe and carried a goatskin bag containing three objects that had been carried away from the home it would never see again.

The first was a little pouch of fine cloth, bound with golden wire. Wrapped in the soft folds were the discarded bones of a dormouse.

The second was a small carved doll, made of finely polished olive wood. It had been used often and so well loved that it was never passed down to the three younger sisters who had begged for it in vain. The third was a fairly small, incredibly flat and smooth rectangle of darkness. From time to time, incomprehensible images of the future would reveal themselves in the surface if she stared deeply into it.

By the time the vultures found the captain's head, lashed to the top of the mast, the passenger had disappeared over the dunes and vanished into the oak forests, moving in eerie silence. But it could not have been the High-Born, not at all. For her parents had told all the Lupines who lived in their region that their eldest daughter had been married off to a nice wolf-boy from a respectable pack in far away Hybla Magna. They spoke of her less and less often as the years went past. Eventually, they ceased mentioning her altogether and her younger sisters recalled her only vaguely. Their attentions were turned toward other things, greater events that were rumored to put human nations and kingdoms in peril; attentions that threatened *anutsim* lives of quiet, hidden comfort.

In a distant land, it was said, there was a new power, a growing empire built of blood and bronze. As if conjured from the depths of an unholy dream mirror, this was an empire of war, of will, and of worship – an empire of wolves.

ROMAE·CIƆIƆCCLXX
From the Collections of
Prof. Ophelia Archibald

Origins of the *Sarthandor*

by J.H. Archibald*

The term *sarthandor* is commonly used to describe the organized campaign against wolf-men that swept through Europe beginning in the 17th century. In the Lupine language, the word itself means "storm-of-flame," inspired by the raging wildfires that the migrating packs encountered as they passed through drought-stricken regions in their flight from their ancestral homeland.

Although Lupines took great care to remain hidden from humans following the end of the Western Migration – with a few rare exceptions – their existence could not remain secret forever. Myths and rumors spread, faint memories lingered, and stories were told of strange travelers with glowing eyes who could not be hurt by ordinary weapons. Whispers of the 'wolves-in-disguise who walk among men' passed from generation to generation, spawning fabulously terrifying and mostly false tales of bloodthirsty werewolves.

Beginning in 1605, during the first years of James I's reign, sporadic reports and sightings of transformed Lupines became more common throughout England, Scotland, and Wales. Panic took hold in the rural districts of southern England as mobs formed to dispense vigilante justice upon suspected werewolves. Professional "wolf-hunters" took to hunting for trophies under the light of the full moon(though it is believed they killed many more human outcasts than actual wolf-men). As violent and disturbing as these episodes were, they were mere hints of what was to come.

It all began on a pleasant day in April 1620, when King James I went before Parliament to give a speech regarding "wer-woolfes and warlockes living in sundrie and diuerse places in Our Faire

---

*Previously submitted to the *American Journal of Lupinology*. (Rejected.)

Kingdom, disguised in skins stolen from righteous men."

This was an unusual choice for James I, who was thought of as a poor speaker. His address stunned the assembly, running on for over three hours, but delivered with tremendous vigor and a boundless, manic energy. The audience was transfixed; scribes struggled to keep up with the torrent of words; but when they were done, they had recorded an incredible piece of propaganda that had at once cleverly distilled every lie and hateful slander about Lupines that had ever been circulated *and* laid out a plan to root out all accused or suspected, thereby cleansing the kingdom of "the scourge and staine of wer-woolfes."

Many of the claims that James I made were inventively gruesome, particularly his insistence that Lupines practiced human sacrifice, effectively stealing infants and tearing them apart to honor "a daemonic thinge of darkness, a living shadowe, ring'd with cruell teeth and driven by boundless hunger." His knowledge in other areas was distressingly accurate – particularly those regarding the use of silver and fire to control and kill Lupines. The plan he described was chillingly well thought out, involving record-keeping and documentation on a tremendous scale, coupled with the development of a new administrative network of agents who would be responsible for scouring every town, village, and hamlet, leaving nothing to chance. The cost was not small, but the result, he declared, would be worth the effort.

James' unusual eloquence and charm left no doubt about the outcome. Parliament overcame its tremendous antipathy to him, a despised monarch they had recently been more inclined to behead than to listen to, and voted unanimously to provide all the funds he requested and all the authority required to begin the work. Within a month his red-frocked Royal Agents were riding out into the countryside. What followed was an unthinkable tragedy, with public burnings, uprooting of packs from their dens, and wholesale slaughter of those Lupines who were caught before they could flee. Few dared to fight back, conditioned to believe that violence against humans was forbidden by the Edict while others believed that striking out would only justify the massacres and make the situation worse. Fortunately, a reasonable number managed to escape on boats that sailed for the New World colonies. From that day forward, England was forever known to Lupines as "The Empire of Agonies."

Over the next two centuries, the terror of the *sarthandor* spread far and wide, leaping from one country to the next. Aging monarchs and embattled governments across Europe used the fear of Lupines as an excuse for all manner of abuses, such as putting down human rebellions or reinforcing their weakening monarchies by calling on religious authorities for support against the "devil wolves." From the Italian peninsula to the Nordic region, all of them, in quick succession, adopted the strategy laid out by James I – all but one that is. France was the very last to adopt 'la méthode Anglaise' and it wasn't until 1789 that the *sarthandor* was finally embraced by the Bourbon dynasty. An infantry officer, one Maréchal Pétain was promoted and asked to develop a manual and an organization dedicated to the capture of Lupines. King Louis XVI approved it and it became national policy only a few months before he was deposed.

The utility of the *sarthandor* and its methods were not lost on Napoleon I. He and his immediate successor kept Petain's infrastructure and techniques largely intact, but the focus shifted when one of his finance ministers realized that enslavement of Lupines for financial gain was economically preferable to killing them. Realizing that wolf-men could perform heavy labor for long hours under conditions that would kill most humans, special prison-factories were formed for casting heavy cannon, armor plate, and gasworks to power the locomotives, airships, and ironclads that had started to proliferate. Governed and guarded by brutal sadists who would not hesitate to use instruments of both physical and psychological torture to intimidate and control their charges, the worst of these prison-factories found its terrible home on a small island off of Malta. Soon, its name became synonymous with horror among wolf-men everywhere: Ephæstia.

In theory, Ephæstia should have been a delightful place, an island paradise set in the azure blue of the Mediterranean. Instead it was the site of bleak suffering and atrocities. Gray, forbidding stone walls rose up on all sides of the island and a huge smokestack sooty clouds courtesy of a hellish furnace that ran day and night in the bowels of the facility. Inside the gates, all exits were blocked with steel-reinforced bars, all guards armed with silver-studded clubs, and each inmate subjected to intimidation, brutality and the constant threat of being fed to the furnace. It has been said that many of the bullets fired by the conquering French armies were made, quite literally, with the blood and bones of the wolf-men imprisoned on that island of suffering.

Ephæstia operated for seven terrible years, gorging on pain and disgorging armaments and smoke, until one October day in 1834. Unknown to the French command, a small squadron of ships had sailed up from the North African coast, maneuvering at night under cover of fog. To the amazement of the guards on duty, mysterious ships loomed from the mist and unleashed a blistering barrage of cannon-fire while a squadron of highly disciplined troops staged a swift landing.

Led by the flagship *Liberator*, commanded by Captain James

Laurence, they had come all the way from the other side of the world to put an end to Ephæstia. The Wolf Marines of the American Expeditionary Force stormed the prison gates and overwhelmed the garrison, freeing hundreds of prisoners who would return in the holds of the no-longer mysterious ships to live in the United States.

That victory marked the official end of *sarthandor.* Two decades later, the British government began the 'Rapprochement' policy which began to allow Lupines to return to the lands they had fled so long ago. Today, those returned wolf-men live in most of the countries of Europe – albeit in very small numbers – under a variety of legal protections that grant them nearly all the same rights as human beings.

It is fair to say that the 20th century promises to be a far more enlightened era than any the world has ever seen before. Man and wolf-man are finally at peace and we have put the chaos and cruelty that began with James I behind us, at long last.

N.B.: It should be noted that many of the Wolf Marines who participated in the 1834 raid at Ephæstia, liberating the last of the *sarthandrim* and ending their long nightmare of captivity, were descendents of the same Lupines who had been driven out of England two hundred years earlier.

The Curious Tale of
Little Red
Raging Hood

Once, in a time when humanity was wracked by epidemics of fear and the world was beset by the turmoil of war, a peaceful valley lay apart from it all, nestled between the guarding walls of high mountains.

In that place, no armies clashed, no mobs sought victims by torchlight, and no inquisitors exacted righteous vengeance in the name of deity or despot. The secluded valley was serene and beautiful, though its serenity was a lonely one and its beauty melancholy. Every sound in the valley, from the gurgling splash of the streams to the wind in the boughs of the ancient forest, seemed like a sigh of longing.

The lands beyond had been bright and welcoming once, but no more. Life beyond its walls had become hard and unforgiving. Only the valley's serenity remained untouched by the cruelty which infected the world. It was a timeless sliver of peace, drifting slowly into the warmth of myth.

In the valley, sleek rainbow trout jetted through snow-melt pools and streams; like living gems, they glittered and dove in the crystal clear water. Small herds of swift roe-deer ran in the deep glades, always alert for predators who might enjoy a meal or two of venison. Fat, chirping marmots weaved and dodged the eternal attentions of sharp-eyed eagles on the high meadows.

And then, of course, there were three other inhabitants, dwelling in a pair of tiny cottages, one on each end of the valley floor. The great forest separated the tidy homesteads. Only a thin, wavering path beneath the overstory suggested their connection.

One of the cottages was home to a little maid and her mother. The little maid's elderly grandmother lived in the other. The three of them were fortunate indeed to live amongst such beauty. Every day, they witnessed the splendor of the forest, the quicksilver song of the streams, and the fierce majesty of the mountains that shielded them from the harms of the outside world.

Though the valley was a sanctuary from the outer world, seasons and storms still intruded. Summers were all too brief, winters were much too long, and all who lived there had to toil hard, each and every day.

Gathering food, keeping their cottage walls daubed, patching their roofs against rain, and mending their clothes demanded much of them. They lived without fear of the violence and turmoil that raged outside, but the three who sheltered in the valley had to work hard; mother, grandmother, and little maid.

Now it might be supposed that the little maid suffered terribly in her loneliness, for there was scant rest and no chance for friends or play. It is true, she wanted friends, but she did not suffer. Despite the hardship and the lack of comfort and ease, the maid was happy, and found moments of joy and pleasure in her simple life. She took special delight in walking the path to her grandmother's, who was very old and wise and could see many things that others could not.

Although the old one lived by herself on the other side of the great forest she was not lonely, for she was never really alone. The spirit ancestors, echoes of the ancient bloodline from which she was descended, often came to her and kept her company. She conversed with them in long-dead languages, smiling and laughing at the mystical secrets that they told her. Some she shared, whispering and smiling, with her little granddaughter.

Once every fortnight, the mother sent her young daughter through the great forest to her grandmother's cottage, to wake her if she had gone into one of her trances, to bring her a basket of food, and to make sure the path to her door was clear of leaves and fallen branches.

The old one doted on her granddaughter and gave her what few gifts she had to give. When the little one was tall enough, her grandmother gave her a bright red cloak with a deep, pointed hood. Honored by the special gift, she always wore it and so came to be called Little Red Hood.

One morning, when the falling leaves swirled and the first traces of frost could be seen in the trickling streams, Little Red Hood's mother said, "Arise! Put on your cloak and go see to your grandmother. Wake her from her trance if she needs to be woken, clear the path to her cottage if it is littered with fallen leaves and branches, and take along this basket. I have filled it with food and healing herbs to help her through the coming winter."

The scent of snow rolled down to the valley from tall peaks that gleamed like fangs in the sharp sunlight. High overhead, a pair of dark-winged birds whirled and soared under the clouds, croaking out ominous warnings and brushing the ground with corpse-shadows as they passed. Yet Little Red Hood had no cares for warnings or shadows, so happy was she for the chance to see her grandmother.

She started from the cottage with a skipping step and a song on her lips, but before she could go far, her mother summoned her back with a stern and serious warning.

"Little Red Hood, come here," her mother called from the doorway, watching the dark shapes in the sky with a frown. "Before you go, listen carefully to what I tell you."

"Yes, mother. I am listening," Little Red Hood replied cheerfully.

"Stay in the middle of the path, walk quietly, and do not stray, no matter what interesting or pretty things you may see," she warned.

"Yes, mother," Little Red Hood nodded. "I will stay on the path.""Do not stop to talk to anyone you should meet, no matter how kind they may seem," she continued, "for there have been reports from the other valleys, strangers seeking a way in from the lands beyond the mountains."

"No, mother," Little Red Hood agreed. "I won't talk to anyone." And she wondered about the other valleys, the strangers, and the lands beyond.

"No matter what may happen, keep your destination a secret," she continued, "for our secrets are our survival."

"Yes, mother," Little Red Hood nodded, "I will tell no one of my destination and I will keep all our secrets." With that, she set off into the forest while her mother watched carefully from the doorstep.

As she began her journey, Little Red Hood minded her mother's instructions carefully. She walked in the middle of the path, stayed completely silent, and revealed nothing of her destination. The entrance to the trail was well lit by rays of bright autumn sunshine that shone through the trees. The only noises were the sounds of the winding streams that

danced through the valley floor and the whistle of the wind tumbling the last leaves from the branches. Mischievous squirrels, chipmunks, and wood-mice scampered away as she approached, hiding in the branches, squeaking, and rustling in the fallen foliage as they hunted for food to get them through the approaching winter.

She smiled at their antics, but she did not stop to chase them, no matter how much they squeaked, for she was mindful still of her mother's words and on she went.

oon, the path turned from the streams and sunlit patches and plunged into the shadowy heart of the forest. The rays of sunshine became dimmer and more scattered and the limbs of the great trees more gnarled, reaching up to blot out the light.

Little Red Hood did not like this part of the forest and her pace quickened as she went along. She strode briskly and with purpose, right in the middle of the trail. On and on she walked, until at last she came up to a small clearing.

Here, an ancient grove stood off to one side of the trail, marking a place where grandmother said the spirit ancestors tarried in their journeys between their world and the world of the valley. The spirits gathered in this place to transact their secret business, sharing secrets that were beyond imagining, whispering and cavorting out of sight of the living. Little Red Hood's limbs felt cold as she paused there.

She looked upon the grove and shivered, but not from the cold. She felt eyes upon her and their gaze was not wholesome. Pulling her cloak tight around her shoulders, she was about to quicken her pace when she noticed something, a bright and lively splash of color lying on the ground.

A sweet scent carried by the cold breeze drew her in, enticing her to step off the path. As she walked closer and closer, she saw that it was a beautiful flower, richer and redder than anything she had ever seen. It was a rose, deeper and more vibrant than any flower that had ever grown in the valley, even more beautiful than her own beloved cloak.

She stooped to pick it up, but a winged shadow passed

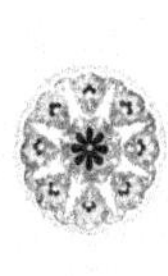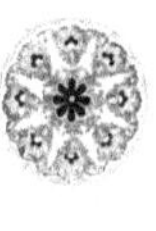

overhead and a harsh call stopped her in her tracks. A bird swooped low over the treetops. She could see its feathers were the deep black of the nighttime sky, as dark as the spaces between the stars, with a streak of white on each wing.

ll at once, a sweet and kindly voice called out to her, "Good morning, Little Girl." Little Red Hood was startled, but unafraid. She did not think that any wicked thing could have so kindly a voice, so she turned towards it and smiled.

"What is your name, Little Girl?" the man's voice called out, sweetly.

"I am called Little Red Hood, if you please, sir," came her reply. She curtseyed, as she had seen the princesses and fine ladies do in the books that she read in her grandmother's cottage.

"And what have you got in your basket, Little Red Hood?" called the voice.

"Food and healing herbs, sir. My mother packed it herself."

At that there was a rustling in the foliage and out stepped a tall, thin man wearing boots which had been polished into a brilliant shine. He was dressed in a crisp, elegant uniform, well-worn, but clean and cleverly mended.

A big wolfskin cloak was thrown over the uniform, warm and soft, with fine gray fur. The wolf's head was still attached, pulled up to form a sheltering hood. An old musket was slung over one shoulder and a well-used saber was slung over the other, dangling down to his hip.

The Wolf's Head Was Still Attached

Little Red Hood's mother and grandmother would have known at once that he was a Hunter, well-paid for the bounties he took and quite good at his chosen profession. Little Red Hood did not know this, she only saw the pretty rose and only heard his kind voice. Looking down at Little Red Hood, he smiled and cocked his head to the side.

"Where are you going with this basket, Little Red Hood?" asked the Hunter.

"I am going to my grandmother, sir," she answered

"Where does your grandmother live, Little Red Hood?" She noticed that the eyes of the wolf's-head hood had been sewn closed to keep out the rain.

"She lives at the end of this path, through the great forest, in a little cottage near the foot of the mountains, sir. But it is a long walk from here, as the path winds and curves, so I mustn't tarry."

The Hunter looked at her, with a growing smile, before he said sternly, "No, you mustn't tarry. Get on your way now, Little Red Hood! And please wish your grandmother a good evening from me when you see her."

 ith a rustle and swirl of his wolfskin cloak, he vanished into the trees, leaving Little Red Hood all alone. She stood there for a time, the red rose losing its scent in the chill as she wondered where he was going. She strained her ears to hear him trotting swiftly through the undergrowth, straight into the forest.

As the sounds faded away, she bent down and picked up the red rose, placing it in her basket. There was something strange about the rose that she had not noticed before, another scent that mingled with the sweet perfume, something sour and rotten. She kept it just the same, and continued along the winding trail all the rest of the way through the forest.

The walk seemed longer than usual, the wind seemed colder than it ought for that time of year, and her burden seemed heavier with each step, but she continued onward.

t was late when she finally arrived, chilled and shivering, at the entrance to her grandmother's cottage. The leaves on the doorstep had been brushed aside, as though her grandmother had been expecting someone.

Little Red Hood knocked at the door, and called out:

"Good evening, Grandmother! It is I, Little Red Hood. I have brought you food and healing herbs and here is a red, red rose that I found in the clearing."

A voice called, thin and weak from within the cottage, "Come in, dear, come in. Lift the latch and the door will fly open."

Obediently, Little Red Hood lifted the latch and the door flew open. The room within was dark and she could see nothing. She blinked in the gloom before stepping through the threshold and she closed the door behind her to keep out the chill. Soft darkness washed over her and all was quiet and still.

She moved forward, her eyes adjusting to the low light and saw what she always saw within; a little stove filled with flickering embers and ash, a few old shelves, bare except for some crumbling books, and a big bed, cloaked in thick curtains and piled high with hides and furs. When she stopped to light a candle, the curtains parted and a peering eye looked out inquisitively.

"Grandmother, is that you? Are you awake?" asked Little Red Hood.

"Yes, dear, I am awake," the thin, weak voice replied. "Come closer. Oh! You are shivering with the cold. The

fire has gone out. Why don't you take off your cloak and come get into bed with me and warm yourself."

Shivering, she stepped slowly forward and the voice from the bed said, "Get in, my dear." As she slipped in, her shivering became more intense, and the ancient frame groaned and creaked.

he laid her head down on the thin pillow and a voice spoke in the darkness:

"My, what big ears you have, my child."

"All the better to hear you with, grandmother." The bed continued creaking as Little Red Hood's body shivered and she strained to pull the blankets over her shoulders. Again came the voice out of the darkness next to her.

"My, what big eyes you have, my child!"

"All the better to see you with, grandmother." And in the darkness, Little Red Hood's eyes did appear large and lustrous. As she turned her head on the pillow, the face next to her stared in wonder, for two pale, blue lights flickered deep inside her eyes. Then the voice spoke again:

"But, dear child, what a big nose you have!"

"All the better to smell you with, grandmother," said little Red Hood.

The sound of a breath inhaled through two large nostrils seemed to stir the bedposts themselves as Little Red Hood snuffed up the odors and scents from the body that lay next to her.

The bed now groaned terribly, and even though she held onto the warm covers, they could not cover all of her body. Little Red Hood shuddered, shaking the frame and making the bedposts creak ever more loudly, like the masts of a galleon running before a storm.

"My goodness, child, what a big mouth you have! And such teeth!"

ittle Red Hood's lips parted to reveal her mouth, full of teeth now grown long and deadly, for the young maid had grown and changed. Her ears were large and pointed, her eyes glared with an icy-blue light, her nose extended to a long, sharp snout, her skin had grown a pelt of soft, silky fur and her arms and legs had transformed into long, terrible limbs tipped with vicious claws that reached out for the Hunter.

Little Red Hood bared her teeth, razor-edged and hungry and she howled out:

"What have you done with my grandmother?"

But before she could seize the Hunter, he rolled out of the bed and scuttled away like an insect into the darkened corner.

Frightened, he jostled Little Red Hood's basket, revealing its bloody contents and spilling them out, drip-drip-dripping onto the cottage floor, staining the rose an even deeper shade of red. Little Red Hood jumped from the bed landing in a crouch on all fours, snarling in anger at his deceit.

The scent of blood and a howling wolf-like form seemed to jar the Hunter from his fearful stupor and he grabbed his loaded musket from behind the door, ready to take one of the three trophies he had come to the valley to claim.

Little Red Hood's sharp nose caught the scent of the silver bullet in his musket, its muzzle now pointed directly at her heart. Though the hands that held the weapon trembled, the Hunter had fired it many times before and he would not miss his target.

Sensing this, Little Red Hood gathered herself to leap, determined that if she must die, she would end the Hunter's life before she went to join her spirit ancestors. The Hunter's practiced finger began to squeeze the trigger and the icy-blue light in Little Red Hood's eyes shone out fiercely as she roared her defiance.

Little Red Hood Gathered Herself to Leap

At that moment, the latch on the cottage door lifted, and the door tore away from its hinges. Little Red Hood's grandmother appeared, swift and deadly, uttering a frightful roar through gaping jaws.

Before the hunter could pull the trigger, Grandmother was upon him, tearing his head from his body with one-two swipes of her ancient claws. The severed head rolled across the floor and was promptly stopped by the corner bedpost.

And that was the end of the Hunter.

Little Red Hood was saved, and she yelped with joy, but the night was far from over. Her grandmother had much to share with Little Red Hood. The young wolf-maid had only just begun to appreciate the Gift, so she spent the night with her grandmother, prowling in the forest and talking to her ancestors of long, hard migrations, of hunts for the great, shaggy beasts that once walked the earth, and of the love and loyalty of pack, the sacred duty to protect the weak and outcast, and the many blessings of Mother Luna.

As the Hunter's moon faded with the dawn, she journeyed back across the woods to tell her mother the tale and relate everything that she had learned.

And That Was the End of the Hunter

For the rest of her life, she always minded her mother and kept her secrets for the sake of herself and for those who would come after her.

From that day forward, she came to be known as 'Little Red Raging Hood' and one day, she taught her own cubs this important lesson:

Obey your elders, listen well,
Though I be old and gray,
The foes I fought and vanquished once,
May come again some-day.
So please remember, cub of mine,
These words of sages wise;
Our predator becomes our prey
When those who kneel arise!
We creep and stalk when e'er they come,
They shall not take my hide,
For these green valleys are our homes,
With forests deep and wide;
I bid you cub, be cunning,
And deft stratagems devise,
Make prey of all our predators,
And upward we shall rise!

The Monster, The Mayor
- and -
the Merchant

Translator's Note

This story is relatively modern, dating to the late 18th century. Oddly, it has no Lupine characters. Although it is quite obviously a work of purest fiction, it may have been inspired by an actual event.

In 1773, a report from the Grand Duchy of Hendrich-Baïsen mentions that a large animal was seen rampaging through the countryside, later captured, determined to be "of demonic origin," and condemned to death.

Further specifics are sadly lacking, but this incident might have been recorded by humans and embellished later, ultimately becoming a Lupine cautionary tale in the form of an exaggerated parody of the actions of men.

My queries to the author, Miss March, have yielded only silence so far, but I must ask - is this story the work of men or wolf-men?

-J.H.A.

Author's Reply

I thank Mr. Archibald once again for his excellent translation, for he has again produced something exceptional.

As for his continued questions, it amuses me to know he divides the world into such neat, simple categories. Up or down; yes or no; man or wolf-man – are these the only available dimensions in his universe?

Although I am afraid I can't help him with that, I can offer the following:

I present this tale for reasons that are entirely my own.

Whoever wrote it down and however it came to be – both questions of very limited significance, in my opinion – understand that this story is not yet finished.

In the aftermath of fire, the warmth of destruction may give rise to something new. Watch closely and you will see that deep in the ashes, something stirs...

-J.M.

any years ago, on a warm summer morning, a bear emerged from the depths of the Sachsenwald forest. Stepping out of the leafy shadows, it blinked in the bright sunlight, sniffed the air carefully, and began walking towards the distant city of Lünaborg a t a steady pace.

It did not take very long for the human inhabitants of the region to take notice of the bear and its destination. In no time at all, word had spread far and wide, causing tremendous alarm. It was clear that this was not just an average, everyday sort of bear. Three specific things about it whipped everyone around Lünaborg into a frenzy.

First of all, it did not seem to have the usual bear-like obsession with food, for it passed right by any number of orchards, fields, and barns without making any attempt to stop and gorge itself on the bounties within. Neither was it the least bit bothered by the presence of humans, becoming neither frightened nor aggressive when it saw them out on the road. It did not stop to maul them or to snap their spines in two like so many dry twigs. In fact, instead of curling back its lips and roaring at them, it merely offered a bemused smile and a polite nod – as if wishing them a good day – and continued walking down the road, as though it had far more important matters to attend to. And yet, as shocking as the beast's gentle temperament and purposeful gait were, the primary cause for the hysteria that engulfed Lünaborg was not the bear's behavior, but its size.

The truth of the matter was that this bear was the most enormous one of its kind that had ever been seen before, not just in the last few years or decades or centuries, but *ever*. It was astonishingly huge, a living mountain of flesh and bone, and in the opinion of all who saw it, it was much, much larger than any bear, or indeed, any land-dwelling animal had any right to be. Perhaps, if any of the witnesses had been on hand two thousand years earlier to see Hannibal's mammoths smash through the gates of Rome or had witnessed the thundering rampage of the dreaded Indrik Beast, they might have had something to compare it to. Lacking that reference, they simply said it was like ten regular bears rolled into one and big as a cathedral, if a cathedral had stout legs and thick, brown fur.

No matter its size, all through the morning, the ursine giant walked on towards the city. It paused very briefly a few times at the farm houses along the way and appeared to listen with grave concern to the sobs of the terrified families huddling inside. The bear could have easily broken down the doors or torn off the thatched roofs and enjoyed a bloody buffet of peasant flesh, but it did nothing of the sort. Instead, it made a series of soft huffs and grunts which sounded oddly benevolent and strangely calming; an apology of sorts to those who dwelt within, then it continued on its way.

Later that morning, the local militia from Lünaborg went to intercept the bear and shoot it before it could harm anyone else. Their captain marched them out double-time, stopping only so that he could enjoy a light lunch, an aperitif or two, and get a quick haircut. Finally, when he was satisfied that he looked adequately heroic, he bravely positioned himself well to the rear of his troops, and commanded them to deliver a decisive blow so that he could ride back to the city and win another medal.

His men stood obediently at attention in the hot sun, trying to look fierce and decisive. Unfortunately, it took a long while for the bear to actually show up, which everyone felt was very inconsiderate given how hot it was. When it did finally arrive, it gave the regiment an embarrassed wink and sat down in the road with an expectant look.

The captain, shocked to see that the reports of this monster's size had not been exaggerated, lost no time giving the order to fire. Crack, crackle, crack went the muskets! Volley after volley, a shower of lead whizzed through the air and struck the bear, for it was so large that even the Lünaborg militia couldn't miss. But alas! Not one bullet out of the hundreds that were fired did any harm, for they couldn't pierce the bear's thick hide.

The bear waited for a while, but eventually, after all the soldiers had had a chance to shoot it a few times, it got up and continued its journey, approaching the long lines of terrified men with a genial twinkle in his eye and what might have been a forgiving smile. The entire regiment immediately lost their nerve, broke ranks and fled.

The bear did not give chase or bother the soldiers in any way, though it did stop to take a close look at the captain who had fallen from his horse after fainting. Pausing to admire the excellent job that the captain's barber had done, the bear gave a rumble of apology to the unconscious man and gently licked his powdered face with a tongue the size of a wagon wheel. With that, he continued onward.

When news of these awful events reached Lünaborg, the response was nothing less than frenzied chaos. Scattered rumors of soldiers defeated, their brave captain dead, and a dozen men swallowed whole as they tried to flee were soon accepted as verified fact. An angry mob formed, marched to the mayor's house, and demanded that he take action.

"That monster-bear is coming!" cried the people. "It's a bloodthirsty demon that has killed scores of men, women, and children, bringing destruction and death to all. Do something!"

Now, whatever else he might have been, the mayor of Lünaborg was actually very clever. He had ridden out earlier that day in secret and gotten a good look at the bear through his official mayoral telescope. He realized immediately that it was actually very gentle, and, if anything, less dangerous than most of the human inhabitants of Lünaborg. At the same time, he knew his tenure as mayor might come to a very abrupt end if he said anything of that sort to the mob that had assembled that day, prepared as they were with pitchforks, scythes, and torches.[1] Since he really enjoyed living in the mayoral mansion, riding in the mayoral coach, and wearing his golden chain of office – not to mention having an unsevered mayoral neck upon which to hang said chain – he thought very, very quickly. Within moments he had a plan...

"Brave citizens of Lünaborg," he shouted at the top of his voice, "I salute you, for despite the lies you have been fed by your so-called leaders, you have finally seen the truth! It is not merely a bear, but a demonic hellbeast, headed here to tear our strongest men limb from limb, bruise our most beautiful women, turn our obedient, devout children into gnostics and vegetarians, and destroy our beloved Lünaborgian way of life. But worse than that, the bloated plutocrats that rule this town have tried to hide it from you!"

While a few members of the mob exchanged puzzled glances, the mayor went on to declare that this was obviously a *foreign* bear, not like the good, patriotic local bears who knew how to die when they were shot. As the crowd warmed up to this bizarre fabrication, he went on.

"The truth is that this bear, though violent and devious, is at heart nothing but a weak, sniveling coward," he suggested, hoping that

---

[1] Lünaborg's mobs had lots of practice rounding up suspected werewolves, witches, and people with funny accents.

attacks of moral character would prevent anyone from wondering how a creature could be weak and sniveling, but simultaneously capable of biting grown men in half. "It couldn't possibly have defeated our brave militia all on its own. So it must have had help from corrupt, greedy traitors who have been deviously, um, hang on... yes, lurking. These bear-loving, devious lurkers are in the pay of foreign potentates who hate our city and all that it stands for. Now give me your support and I will set everything right, restoring Lünaborg to greatness again once more!"

A huge cheer went up at this. The mayor smiled, wiped the anxious sweat from his brow and went right to work. First, he rounded up all the philosophers, itinerant scholars, freethinkers, and other evildoers and threw them in jail. Then, he hired dozens of mercenaries and had them move the giant brass cannon that stood in the town square[2] out to the city gates. A hundred volunteers were pressed into service to weave a giant net that would, at the appropriate moment, be affixed to a hoist composed of a complex system of pulleys and levers. Another hundred were sent to carefully lay out seven huge chains, covering them with leaves and branches.

They had just finished their preparations when the bear finally appeared. It caught the scent of the waiting mob and saw them hiding behind the wall, but it did not run away. Instead, it came forward and sat down right in the middle of the road, tilted its head and shrugged as if to say "Well, what are you waiting for?"

At this, the mayor gave the signal and the cannon was fired with an earsplitting BOOM! A massive cannonball struck the bear square in the chest, but it did no damage. Instead it bounced right off without causing the least bit of harm. It bounded for almost half a mile before it was successfully halted by the walls of a nearby

---

[2]Formerly the die in a well-regarded and somewhat famous peace memorial in old Lünaborg.

orphanage, killing the twenty or so unfortunates within and causing slight scratches to the valuable cannonball. Meanwhile, two hundred men hauled hard on the ropes and pulleys, sending a vast web of netting over the bear before wrapping the chains tightly around it. Although it could easily have shrugged off all the bindings, then stomped each and every human present into a damp, bloody smear, it simply waited, mild and patient as ever.

With the help of a dozen great draft-horses, and with much sweating and swearing, the men dragged the captured bear into the town square and congratulated each other on their bravery. A celebration was held in honor of the mayor's triumph with barrels of beer for the heroes to drink and tiny flags for the children to wave. All the townspeople kept a careful distance from the captive animal, staring at it in wonder and toasting the mayor's health as the council went off to decide the bear's fate.

The great bear sat patiently, chained in the square outside the council hall, listening to the debate inside. The mayor and his councilors were now arguing about how to best kill the troublesome bear that they had so expertly captured. Guns were clearly useless against it and hanging was out of the question. A professional executioner with specialized experience in killing would probably be required, but it dawned on them that the expense would be enormous.[3]

No one on the council had any idea how they could possibly afford to kill it, they

certainly couldn't keep it, nor could they let it go. The idea of asking the wealthiest citizens of the town to donate the money was briefly considered, but swiftly set aside as all the wealthiest citizens were on the council. Tempers frayed soon thereafter and someone accused the mayor of dooming the city to bankruptcy with his

---

[3]In those days, executioners charged by the pound.

mad bear schemes and insane bear manias. Eyebrows were raised, insults were traded, beards were pulled, just as the scuffle threatened to turn into a fracas, a mysterious figure carrying a large sack suddenly appeared on the far end of the hall and announced to the struggling figures…

"Gentlemen, I come seeking his honor, the Mayor. I've a business proposition!"

Everyone in the hall froze, mid-fracas. The mayor, being the quickest thinking of the combatants, straightened out his robes, let go of the council secretary's beard, and demanded that the stranger explain himself. Who was he and why was he interrupting their solemn deliberations?

The new arrival walked into the hall and received a thorough appraisal from all present as they tried to determine if he was someone important. His clothes were quite elegant and well-fashioned and all his accouterments, from the rings on his fingers to the heavy pocket-watch in his waistcoat declared him to be a man who had achieved success. Yet despite his tailoring and evident wealth, it was apparent to all of them, based on the absence of a sword at his side and the lack of emblems on his person, that while he might be rich, he was no nobleman. No aristocratic blood flowed in his veins, and he could claim no titles.

So the mayor thought to himself: "Well, then this intruder is merely a merchant, albeit a rich one. He's not from around here, he's carrying gold, and he wants something…" And in the mayor's mind, the stranger went from "possible predator" to "probable prey." He offered a broad smile that looked almost sincere and welcomed the man to Lünaborg, asking how they might be able to help him.

The man spoke well, but his accent was unrefined and his hands were those of a peasant, callused and sullied by actual work. The merchant explained he had come from Vindobona, having made his money in trade, but he was tired of constantly haggling and bartering – and now he had a marvelous idea for a new venture. He had just leased a large tract of land outside the city walls, and there he intended to build a new wonder that would transform Lünaborg...

"An arena!" he announced, entranced with his own vision. "A theater to show spectacles that will fascinate and delight everyone, old and young, rich and poor. Races, concerts, oratories, but most of all – fights between the most astounding beasts that have ever walked the globe; striped tigers from the far eastern jungles of Indrus, lions from the equatorial deserts of Kemet, giant eagles from the high Kakaz mountains, and – if any can still be found – maybe even a savage wolf-man or two. The more ferocious and terrifying, the better, I'll put them in the ring and let the crowds thrill to the sight." He strode about, unable to sit still, as he kept on talking.

"The crowds will come first out of curiosity, yes, but if I am to keep them coming back, week after week, I'll need a champion, an animal so large and powerful, they'll never tire of watching it roar and rage. It must be a unique, powerful, and unstoppable killer. Like this man-eating bear I've just seen outside. Incredible! I must have it, no matter what. So name your price for that monster, I'll pay it."

The mayor, trying hard not to giggle, praised the merchant for his vision and bold spirit while signaling frantically to the other councilmen to keep quiet until they had taken every last coin they could get from the idiot. He knew very well that the bear sitting outside in the square would never fight anything, but he showered the merchant with praise, bargained a little for the look of the thing, and accepted the giant bag of money with hands that hardly shook at all. How fortunate, it seemed that the merchant had brought just enough to pay for the bear, along with the permits and taxes required to build a... what was it again? Oh, yes, an arena. Clerks were summoned and documents were drafted accordingly.

Fifteen minutes later, with the ink on the bill of sale still drying, the merchant strode out into the square and gave orders to a waiting retinue of laborers, animal trainers, and expert bear-baiters who carted his new prize bear off to the great stone structure that continued to rise just outside town. The merchant had paid half his fortune to build it, and now he paid the other half for the great bear. As the laborers carefully lowered the bear into the deep pit that had been built to contain it, the merchant danced with joy at the thought of all the money he would make and the glory his new prize would win him in his shining, monumental arena...

After all, what could possibly go wrong?

Three weeks later, it was clear that everything had gone terribly wrong. The building of the arena was progressing incredibly slowly. After all their promises of support for the new endeavor, the city council of Lünaborg had principally been concerned with finding ways to extract even more money from the merchant. The local quarries gladly sold him stone, but at twice the ordinary price. Sawmills welcomed him warmly whenever he came to purchase timber, adding an extra zero to his bill. Carters overcharged him, masons and builders gouged him, and tax gatherers flocked like vultures. Yet despite the toll it took on the merchant's coffers, these daylight robberies were far less concerning than the truth about the prize monster he had purchased.

The horrible truth was that his giant killer bear would not kill. In fact, while it seemed quite content to rest and relax in the deep, well-constructed pit, it showed no inclination to commit aggression. The trainers had tried everything they could think of to get it riled up, from throwing pebbles at it, to shouting at it, to poking it in the ribs with long poles while it slept. Hot embers only seemed to tickle the bear while buckets of icy water seemed to refresh it. Even the nest of angry hornets the trainers dropped into the pit only buzzed harmlessly around the animal, landing occasionally on its nose and paws to pay their respects before flying away with a grateful buzz.

There was one moment of excitement when they tried banging on drums and blowing whistles, for the bear not only woke up, but actually got up on its hind legs and waved its huge paws in the air. This glimmer of hope had all of the trainers cheering at first, thinking they had finally roused the bear. Soon, however, they realized that rather than stomping in rage, it was *dancing*. It waltzed around the pit in a clumsy, arrhythmic shuffle, until everyone was so surprised, they dropped their drums and whistles and started muttering and shaking their fists at the animal, still lost in the reverie of the dance. The men turned red with embarrassment and fury and cries of "Stupid bear!" and "You're a terrible dancer!" filled the air as they vented their frustration.

The bear's reaction to these insults was startling and so upset them that the head trainer went to the merchant to complain on behalf of his men.

"Very sorry, sir, but I don't think we can take much more of this. I've worked with every sort of fighting animal you could think of

– bulls, leopards, hyaenas, ground sloths, flesh-eating ostriches – but I've never seen anything like that bear," said the head trainer, sheepishly, clutching his hat nervously. "It's horrible."

"What are you talking about?" the merchant said, suspiciously. "Just yesterday you told me the only way it would ever kill anything would be if it sat on top of it by accident. Did something happen?"

"In a way, yes sir. Today was not a good day, sir. Not a good day at all. The men were all very tired and, well, they got upset and started swearing and calling the bear names. That got to it, I think, for it turned right around faced us all and, and…"

"Yes?" asked the merchant, excitedly. "What happened? Did it rage? Did it roar?"

"No, sir," the head trainer said, miserably. "It looked at us.""Looked at you, how exactly? Was it enraged? Angry?"

"No," the head trainer said, slowly. "Not angry, exactly. Just-"

"Yes?"

"Just disappointed," the head trainer mumbled. He was a simple man who was much better with wild beasts than with words. He couldn't bring himself to say that when the bear had looked at him with its huge, sorrowful, liquid eyes he actually felt guilty, as though his six decades spent goading animals to tear each other to pieces was wrong somehow. The bear's look of woe had shaken him profoundly and made him question many things, including whether it was possible to undo the past. He shivered as an unaccustomed sensation of regret passed through his heart.

The exasperated merchant started to open his mouth to curse the man for a fool, but he stopped. Something in the head trainer's eyes made him rethink his approach and when he spoke again, he tried to be kind, but firm. "Look, maybe we're going about this all wrong. I have an idea…"

The merchant went out the next day and purchased a wild catamount, a spitting, snarling, tawny-skinned terror that had no fear of man. It snarled savagely from inside its cage and nearly took off the head trainer's fingers as it slashed at him through the bars. They carted it back and lowered it carefully into the pit. The bear appeared to be sleeping, but stirred drowsily when the cage bumped on the floor of the pit. When they pulled on the rope that released the cage door, the great cat leapt out and gave a bloodcurdling shriek of rage at the thing in the corner.

"That's right!" the merchant shouted, "go get him! Teach him how to fight!" He slapped the head trainer on the back in a fit of excitement. "This will work, I can feel it." The older man sighed simply saying: "Just wait…"

The shadowy ball of fur in the corner of the pit unfolded itself to stand on its hindlegs. The catamount, not quite at its full height, went immediately quiet and still. It looked up, then much further up. The bear seemed quite pleased to have a visitor and offered a delighted nod and a happy rumble by way of greeting, but its hospitality was unwelcome. The catamount turned around and attempted to make a vertical ascent, right up the sheer stone walls. It nearly died trying to claw its way and in the end, it had to be lassoed and lifted out of the pit, limp and exhausted. The bear looked quite sorry when they took it away.

Despite this dispiriting performance, the merchant would not be dismayed. He tried again and again, buying up every animal he could get his hands on that was even plausibly fierce. There was a procession of snorting boars, three huge crocodiles from Asia Minor, even a supposed werewolf – who was later revealed to be nothing more than an ordinary human hermit who hadn't washed, shaved, or cut his hair in four decades. None of them elicited anything more than a sorrowful look and an apologetic grunt from the bear.

Desperate, the merchant now called in learned men, several whom the mayor had previously driven out of town; dusty-robed scholars and near-sighted savants bearing books and scrolls came and peered down into the pit, transfixed by the enormous face that looked back up at them. None of them had anything to offer that was useful, except one – a monk.

The monk showed up uninvited one afternoon after the merchant had dismissed the rest of the useless scholars, paying them with the very last of his coin. He saw the robed figure by the side of the pit and went to shoo him away. To his surprise, when he looked down into the pit, the bear was not only awake, but standing just underneath the monk with his eyes closed, craning his head towards the new arrival and inhaling deeply through his nose.

"Do you know what kind of bear this is?" the merchant asked, listening to the air whistling through the bear's nostrils. "Are there any more of them out there?"

"No," said the monk in a harsh whisper. The merchant could see only the vague outlines of a face under the enveloping hood. "There isn't another like it anywhere in the world. At least, not many. Not anymore. For the power and majesty of his kindred has waned, soon it will vanish completely under the weight of modernity, disappearing into the mists of-"

"Yes, fine," said the merchant, impatiently. "Nice and poetic. Mythic and lyrical and so forth. But how do I get it to fight? To kill? I'm about to lose my doublet here!"

"Fight?" said the monk, coughing with the effort of speaking in a menacing, throaty whisper. "Don't be ridiculous. This being will not fight and it will never kill. This creature has devoted its last days to peace. Can't you see that?"

To the merchant's great surprise, the bear stood up on its hindlegs at the sound of the monk's voice, peering up intently with a soulful look. If he didn't know any better, the merchant would have said it was a look of true love. He didn't know a great deal about true love, having spent his life buying and selling. In his experience, true love wasn't something that could be bought or sold.[4]

The monk made some strange, subtle gesture at the edge of the pit and the bear dropped back down on all fours, wandered over to a corner, curled up into an enormous ball, and made a noise like a depressed foghorn. The merchant turned to ask another question, but the robed figure had vanished without a trace.

At sunset that day, all the animal trainers resigned, following the head trainer away into a waiting wagon and riding far away from Lünaborg.

"Where are you going?" shouted the merchant at the retreating wagon.

The head trainer wanted to tell him that he had a lot to do, a million acts of contrition to perform and a veritable mountain of dismembered animal corpses to unload from his conscience. He wanted to tell the merchant to leave his failing venture behind and get in the wagon and go with them, to begin the long, long process of cleansing the stains on his soul. But he wasn't one to make long speeches.

"Away from here. Good luck to you, sir..." And he turned around to face west as the wagon disappeared in the light of the setting sun.

---

[4]Rented, maybe, but that isn't the point.

The merchant walked back towards the pit, dejected. Construction had halted at the arena several days prior and the only structure that was actually finished was the bear pit. Word had spread quickly of "the cowardly monster and the foolish merchant," how the well-paid-for beast would not kill anything, even a flea that bit it. Jokes abounded and humorous songs were sung on every street corner in Lünaborg of the pathetic creature and his idiot owner, now bankrupt and sorrowing amidst the ruins of his folly. The merchant's debtors made angry threats, the mayor and the town council sensed that the time had come to finish off their victim, and they used their most vicious weapon…

A lawyer came just as the trainers left, brandishing razor-sharp legal documents. They were covered in dense, impenetrable writing.[5]

"You must vacate the premises in the next few days," he informed the soon-to-be-former owner of the bear. "After that, this animal and this property will be confiscated by the City of Lünaborg and auctioned off to pay your outstanding debts." A squad of town militia stood behind him, bristling with weapons and looking extremely fierce, but keeping a safe distance from the pit.

"Is all of this legitimate?" asked the merchant, as he looked glumly over the heavy stack of documents.

"Oh yes," the lawyer said, snootily. "According to the legal precedent of *'clamant victimae, victores rident[6].'* The sergeant-at-arms will claim the property soon, including that great hairy beast of yours…"

The lawyers, having delivered a mortal blow, retreated. All alone, the merchant sat at the edge of the pit, gazing about the unfinished shell of his arena and wondering where things had

---

[5] It was horrible. There were even codicils.
[6] This phrase, also on the Lünaborg coat of arms, translates to "Winners laugh; Losers weep."

gone so terribly wrong. In a fit of anger he took the papers, flung them into the air and let them flutter down to the floor of the pit. The bear read the entire document with great interest, taking the time to appreciate the devious logic and careful manipulation of established legal precedent. Then, with every sign of enjoyment, he ate each page and waited for nightfall.

The fantastical story of the gigantic bear had traveled far, having even reached the palace where it was whispered carefully into the thin, chilly ears of the Grand Duke himself. Although everyone always praised his excellent sense of humor,[7] this story did not amuse him. His expression alone was enough to send his stewards and marshals scurrying away. A hurried dispatch was made and a coded summons was carried swiftly to a distant, isolated cloister.

That is how, on the same day that the merchant learned he was a pauper, the mayor found himself unexpectedly entertaining a midnight visit from a Holy Quæsitor. Wearing his mayoral robes over his nightshirt, he struggled to explain the half-finished arena on the outskirts of the city, the defacement of the Lünaborg peace memorial, and the general malaise that seemed to have taken

---

[7] Or so said anyone who enjoyed the privilege of breathing.

hold of the townspeople. Even in the grip of panic, the mayor's rambling response was a masterwork of misdirection, aspersion, and evasion. When he finally sputtered to a halt, the Quæsitor gave a reassuring smile and told him that he understood perfectly. It was very clear now where the fault lay, and that he would make sure that everyone got what was coming to them.

The mayor was incredibly relieved, offered a thousand expressions of thanks, and asked the Quæsitor if there was anything else he needed after his long journey to Lünaborg. Food and drink, perhaps? A fine room at one of the city's best inns or hostelries? No, nothing at all, said the Quæsitor, except – might it be possible to go and visit this bear he had heard so much about? The mayor stifled a yawn, and said yes, they could go first thing tomorrow morning. The visitor, still smiling, asked if they could go right away. Something about the way he asked told the mayor it would be a bad idea to decline; and so he tried, without much success, to keep his hands from shaking in the great man's presence.

Had the mayor been thinking rationally, he might have realized that his fears were based on gossip and speculation, not actual knowledge. For instance, he knew that the Society of Quæsitors was very old and very powerful. He knew that the robed men frequently assisted those monarchs and princes whose legitimate rules were troubled by social unrest, heresy and other threats to the natural order, and he knew that they were said to be ruthlessly efficient in their work.

That, however, was all that he knew for sure. Everything else about the Quæsitors, including their numbers, their origins, the location of their headquarters, and their actual relationship to the church was shrouded in mystery. Despite the fact that all he really knew amounted to a handful of vague, unverifiable rumors, the gruesome, bowel-knotting nature of those rumors demanded absolute obedience. And so without stopping to go home and change out of his slippers, the mayor led his distinguished guest out into the night towards the bear pit.

After the lawyers had left, the merchant stomped about until his feet were sore, then went off to lie morosely in the viewing stands for a while, where he attempted to come up with a plan that might halt the impending disaster. He must have nodded off, for he woke up to find it was nighttime. He heard a soft, sad sound coming from the pit. Quietly, he crept toward the sound only to find a robed figure kneeling by the pit, crying inconsolably. The merchant recognized the monk who had spoken to him earlier, still clad in the same robes. The merchant started to demand an explanation for this intrusion, but the monk's hood slipped back, revealing a young head of hair that was not tonsured or shorn, but soft, brown, and long. The monk was a woman, weeping so passionately as she knelt at the edge of the pit that her body shook with the force of her sobs.

The merchant was taken aback, but after a moment's hesitation, he went up to her and put a comforting hand on her shoulder. Before he could ask what had brought her there and why she was crying, he saw something that took his breath completely away. There, in the gloom at the bottom of the pit, he could just make out a man's face looking up at him.

"You fool!" the merchant shouted down. "How did you get down there? You're in terrible danger, we've got to get you out, quickly!"

"Thank you! But may I ask, what danger are you referring to?" the man called up in a pleasant baritone voice. For someone trapped in a dark pit with a giant carnivore, he didn't seem very concerned.

"What danger?" the merchant exclaimed. "Why, the bear, of course. Can't you see it, it's right there in the..."

He trailed off when two things became quickly apparent to him.

The first was that the bear was nowhere to be seen anywhere in the pit. The second was that the eyes of the man seemed very familiar, as was the deeply soulful, loving look he was giving to the crying woman. A question formed on the merchant's lips and he looked from the strange man at the bottom of the pit to the woman and back. The man was incredibly calm, practically blissful, with a thick beard, broad shoulders, and muscular limbs.

He was also completely naked.[8] Like most humans, the merchant was uncomfortable with nakedness, believing that man's natural state involved as many layers of cloth, lace, and leather as there are fig leaves on an ancient tree.

"Who are you?" the merchant finally said, bewildered. "How did you get down there? And where are your clothes?"

"I'm surprised. Don't you recall how I got down here? After all man should know his own property," the baritone voice chuckled. "As for my clothing, I don't often wear any and it's been so long I completely forgot how much you hairless humans care about wearing things like–" The bearded face wrinkled up in the effort to recall the word. "Pints?"

"Pants," said the woman. The merchant was struck by how harsh her voice sounded, how raw and strained it seemed.

"Yes," the man said, "that's it. Well, apologies for my lack of pants, I don't wear them very often. You see, I'm the bear that you purchased. And may I say, I'm very honored to have fetched such a good price."

The merchant was brought out of his shock by this egregious statement. "What's that you say? 'Good price?'" he stammered, furiously. "More like 'wasted fortune!' I could have bought anything with that much wealth – spices, silks, furs, cocoa, tea, a

---

[8]Perhaps if the man's beard had been much longer, his nakedness wouldn't have been an issue.

fleet of ships – and instead, what do I have? An unfinished arena that no one will ever come to and–" he shook his fist at the smiling man. "A naked fool in a pit!"

The naked man's smile didn't falter, but his eyes took on a hard, steely glint in the starlight. He started to speak, intending to offer a gentle retort to the merchant's shouts of anger, but he never had the chance. The merchant suddenly found himself grabbed by the collar and suspended effortlessly over the pit. His boots dangled as the robed woman shook him back and forth.

"How dare you say such things, human!" she growled. "If it wasn't for him, you'd be dead, you and every other dull-eyed, dull-minded brute in this festering dungheap of a city!"

The merchant's eyes bulged and he released a strangled wheeze, partly from surprise and partly because the woman's superhuman grip was draining his life from him. A mournful whimper from the pit made the woman's face soften and she sighed. Reluctantly, she pulled the wheezing merchant back to the edge of the pit and put him down with a thump. He wheezed a few more times and then looked at her in amazement. Finally, he gasped out, "What are you?"

Before the woman could answer there was a shout in the distance and the flicker of torches could be seen coming from the direction of the city. A bell rang out, and the sound of footsteps announced the arrival of the mayor and his visitor with a squad of soldiers serving as escort. The man in the pit called up, in a voice that quavered, but did not break...

"Go now, my beloved one! Go now, and protect our future at all costs. Tomorrow, at sunset, I will rise on the smoke." The merchant, laying on the ground recovering from his airborne adventure, could not see the man in the pit but knew that the merchant could not understand, and it seemed more like the man's visage was wracked with anguish. The woman stood poised, ready to flee, but something held her back. Rage, sorrow, and resignation fought for mastery of her heart, but her voice remained steady and her eyes remained locked on the light of the approaching torches.

"I can't leave you here," she said, "please, enough of this! Just get out of that hole already and let's go back to our den and get on with our lives."

"You know that there is nothing more I want in the world," the man said. "But it cannot be. The vision was very clear; if I go with you, then the madness will come again and this time there will be no stopping it. It will swallow the world whole with poisoned fangs and unhinged jaws. That-Which-Devours will rise, unstoppable, and we will be little more than its playthings. All living things will suffer, the pain and death will be unimaginable. We cannot allow this to come to pass!"

"A vision," the woman said, bitterly. "You're leaving me for a vision – again! Leaving me to deal with everything, all alone – again! Except this time, you're not coming back. I'll have to watch over our home by myself, say the rites by myself, tend to the rituals by myself–"

"You won't be alone this time. Not for long," the man said, very softly and tenderly.

"No, not for long," the woman said, and she reached out with one hand towards the unseen figure below her as if to bridge the gulf between her and the father of the cub she would give birth to in just a few short months.

The torches drew closer and approaching voices could be heard. The man in the pit said something else, but it was in a language the bellow of beasts than the speech of men. To the merchant's surprise, the woman responded in similar fashion. As she did, a powerful gust of wind blew suddenly from the north, carrying with it the scent of snowpack and hoar frost, the frigid blast blew dust and grit into the merchant's face. Squinting and blinking, trying to clear his vision, the merchant thought he saw the woman's eyes glow briefly as her cloak billowed in the wind. With quick, powerful strides, faster than the eye could follow, she vanished into the darkness taking the unseasonable chill with her.

A sergeant-at-arms came forward, ahead of the mayor and his distinguished guest to ensure there was no danger, and found the merchant perched at the edge of the pit, staring into it with a perplexed look. The sergeant heard the man mumbling about women with glowing eyes and bears who were men.

"Witchcraft!" the sergeant-at-arms hissed, and he muttered a charm against witches that his grandmother had taught him.[9] The mayor came next, followed by a newcomer that the merchant had never seen before, noting only that he was quite tall and distinguished-looking, with twinkling eyes and an earnest smile. The merchant was in too much shock, too lost in bewilderment to take notice of the visitor's simple, priest-like vestments that were a very particular shade of red; not a bright, elegant rose-red or a brilliant, playful tulip-red, but a workman-like red, a color peculiar to his unique order. It was the red of blood-spatter and broken skin, the red of exposed organs and crushed spirits; the red of the Quæsitors. The merchant stood to offer words of greeting, but his mind was elsewhere. The Quæsitor stepped closer to get a better look at this man who was too distracted to be afraid of him.

"There is great turmoil in your face, my friend," he said, looking

---

[9]The sergeant's grandmother hated witches and worked hard to develop charms against them. She also knew many spells, brewed potions in her cauldron, and had a nice collection of warts.

closely at the merchant with an expression of sincere concern. "Tell me, what has caused you such turmoil?"

"I was robbed, your honor," the merchant said, addressing the Quæsitor. "It was no bear they sold me, but a man cursed to look like a bear. Or a bear cursed to take the form of a man? I don't know what it is, but it's useless either way and it won't fight like a bear is supposed to. They swindled me, the mayor and his cronies! Me, I'm an honest man, a simple man who wished only to build something for the good people of Lünaborg. But I was taken advantage of with sorcery and tricks! What good is it for honest men like me to build if our dreams are stolen from us?"

The mayor became livid at this, growing red in the face. He took a threatening step towards the merchant and spat back:

"Slander! A deal was struck, a bargain made, papers signed and sealed. Hundreds of Lünaborg's upstanding citizens will testify how you took delivery of that giant animal from us, right in the public square, even made a speech about how your great bear would be a wonder of the world." He paused and smiled nastily before continuing. "Yes, you bought a bear, but what you did with the bear afterwards, who knows? Ha! Even a half-wit like you should have been able to keep track of something that big."

The merchant yelled back, raving about spells and swindles, while the mayor insisted that he had been nothing but fair, and all the while the Quæsitor stood by and listened. He said very little, as a rule, preferring to allow the subjects of his inquiries to fill the spacious silences he offered.

"No bear at all, your grace, just magic and tricks!" the merchant shouted, while the mayor retorted, "Idiot spendthrift! You ruined yourself!" The red-clad man smiled sympathetically and made encouraging nods to both of them, listening as they reached ever-greater heights of rhetorical outrage until the mayor finally collapsed, choking and wheezing on a swollen bolus of hyperbole. The merchant took the opportunity to kneel at the Quæsitor's red-booted feet and plead his case.

"Please your honor, you are a wise man, devoted to the search for the truth. Through the mayor's wicked designs, everything has been taken from me. All I want is my money back, just that. He can even take back this creature, it's probably in on the scheme – do you hear that?" he shouted down into the pit. "You there, naked idiot, I know you're in on this. Come out and show yourself so his grace can see what this sneaky dwarf of a mayor actually sold me."

A shuffling sound in the darkness preceded the emergence of a head, poking out of the shadows. The man in the pit was gone, replaced by the familiar hulking silhouette of the bear. It didn't grunt or snuffle as it sometimes did at the sight of new people, but kept very quiet, tilting its head back and forth at the sight of the Quæsitor. The merchant was dumbfounded.

"I don't understand," he said in a strained voice. "Just a little while ago – I swear to you that was a man!" Still on his knees he grasped the Quæsitor's boot. "You must believe me. Please, your honor…"

Finally the Quæsitor spoke. "Arise, my friend. Please rise." The merchant's heart rose at these words and, taking the Quæsitor's offered hand, he stood. The hand that grasped his was firm and trustworthy and the face he looked up into was friendly and welcoming.

"Do you know what I see in your eyes?" asked the Quæsitor. "I see a good man, a man with a dream who sought to build something. Tell me, please, what was it you wanted to build?"

"A grand arena, like those of antiquity," breathed the merchant, who felt for the first time someone was really listening to him. "A place to stage spectacular fights, races, and performances. It would have been glorious, stupendous, a sort of a magnificent kind of a, um–"

"A monument?" suggested the Quæsitor.

"Yes, your honor!" the merchant enthused. "Just that. A monument."

"Ah, a monument," the Quæsitor nodded happily. "But tell me, please – what would it have been a monument to, exactly?"

Though the question was posed in pleasant, soothing tones, the merchant thought he sensed something underneath the question, something sharp and deadly.

"Not a monument to anything specific," the merchant replied, hesitantly. "Just a place for everyone to come and enjoy themselves, young and old, rich and poor. A place to see something new and forget their troubles for a time."

"Ah, so a monument to earthly thrills and mirth?" The smile on the elderly face widened at this idea and revealed two rows of remarkably strong, incredibly white teeth that were sharper and longer than ordinary. "A monument to joy?"

The merchant tried not to panic and kept on talking.

"Yes, sir, but surely there's nothing wrong with such things, with people coming together and enjoying themselves in a place that welcomes them – is there, your grace?"

"Wrong?" said the Quæsitor with a musical laugh. "Dear friend, nothing an honest man wishes to build is wrong – so long as his soul is free of the infectious rot that makes men turn away from the traditions and values that have kept us from damnation and chaos. Suffering and pain are difficult, but they keep blasphemy from taking hold among the masses." He said no more just then, but turned to look towards the pit. The twin glints of the bear's eyes could just be discerned looking back steadily at him. "Now my friend, are you certain that this is the animal that turned out to be a man in sorcerous disguise? It certainly looks like a bear to me, but I am growing old, of course. My eyes may not be as keen as yours."

"It's a bear and a man, one in the same, your honor!" the merchant insisted. "Such things must be possible. After all, there are still werewolves around, aren't there?"

"Oh yes," said Quæsitor, speaking knowledgeably. "Dirty, nasty things, those werewolves, but mercifully rare now, thanks to the good work of my holy order and many others. But werewolves are very different from – what did you say? A bear that is also a man?"

"Exactly, your holiness. It's a bear now, but just a little while ago, it was certainly a man. And there was a woman, too, I think. She came to see him." The Quæsitor's too-white, too-sharp smile appeared again, but he said nothing. The merchant filled the silence with more nervous words.

"Yes, I'm sure I couldn't have imagined it, your grace. There was a man in the pit and he had no clothes on. He spoke to me, just as clearly as you speak to me now, thanked me for paying such a good price for him! And there was a woman too, most definitely. He said strange things, terrible things to her."

"What sorts of things?" asked the Quæsitor, sharply.

"Things that made no sense. Something about a vision? And madness, a madness which would swallow up the whole world. He called it: 'That-Which-Something?' I can't quite recall..."

"Could it have been 'That-Which-Devours?'" offered the

Quæsitor. "Were those the words your naked man-bear could have said?"

"Yes!" cried the merchant, gratefully. "Oh, your grace. That was it exactly. Thank you! So you believe me then, sir?"

The distinguished, kindly-looking older man grasped the merchant's shoulders and nodded agreeably. "Most assuredly, I believe you. My poor friend! You have been cruelly deceived, toyed with, harmed in the most terrible manner. I am convincednow, beyond all doubt. Justice must be done."

The merchant fell to the ground in relief, uttering thanks and expressing his gratitude in every conceivable way. As tears of joy streamed down his face, the Quæsitor patted him reassuringly on the shoulder before turning to the officer who stood nearby.

"Sergeant, take this poor man and chain him up. Bind him here, in the sight of his profane monument to mirth. He sought to mislead the people, to distract them from their righteous suffering with his merry spectacles of blood. But he is not solely to blame for his failures. It is clear he has been taken advantage of and in his weakness, he was beset by sorcerous and demonic forces."

Before he could protest, the merchant was seized and shackled to a wooden post. The Quæsitor smiled benignly and the mayor could not keep himself from gloating, his smirk breaking into an unseemly grin. It vanished when the Quæsitor placed a hand lightly on his shoulder and ordered the sergeant-at-arms to seize him as well. As he was pinioned and chained next to the merchant, he demanded to be released.

"Why am I being treated just like this vile criminal?" he shouted with the outrage of one who only thought such things happened to other people. "By whose authority do you dare to do this to me, the mayor of Lünaborg?"

The Quæsitor raised an eyebrow very slightly and the mayor shrank back, horrified at his own words. Eventually, the red-clad man stepped closer and put his face down to look right in the mayor's eyes, saying, "I need no authority, other than my own, little mayor. I have full license to do all that is necessary to preserve order, licensed and sanctified by the very highest authority. And in addition to that I have the absolute, unconditional support of the Grand Duke, hereditary master of this miserable place by right of blood and conquest, may he be forever blessed."

"But there must be some mistake," the mayor whimpered. "What have I done?"

"No mistake," came the calm response. "As for what you've done… It is clear that you have gotten too puffed up, too swollen on your own miniscule sense of self-importance. Your actions have brought you and this misguided fool into contact with an unholy, savage animal and now you are tainted with its evil."

"Savage?" said the mayor. "Evil? What are you talking about? It's hopelessly gentle. There's not a trace of anything unholy about it."

"How sad," the Quæsitor said regretfully, "that you have fallen under its spell, unaware and utterly helpless. But don't worry." He turned to look down at the bear one final time. "Tomorrow morning, all will be made right. I will free all of you from these enchantments." He looked down at the merchant. "Don't you wish for that, my friend? Don't you want to be free?"

The merchant, who had slumped down dejected, now looked up and nodded fervently with hope in his eyes. "Free! Yes, your honor, more than anything!"

The Quæsitor leaned down, clasped the merchant's shackled hands firmly, and looked intently at his face. "Spoken like the honest man you are. I must leave to fetch some other friends of mine, but I will return. At sunrise, I promise that you will be freed of the curse of this demon. Better than that, your dream will be realized. The crowds will flock to see what you have built and they will see something marvelous."

"Will they remember it forever?" the merchant sobbed, unable to believe this reversal of fortune.

"Oh yes, I guarantee that they will never forget it." The smile on the face of the Quæsitor was terrifying in its sincerity.

As the merchant sobbed his thanks, the Quæsitor wheeled about on a booted heel and gave the sergeant-at-arms his final orders in a loud, clear voice so that all could hear.

"Sergeant, these prisoners will remain here until tomorrow morning, under constant guard. Then, at dawn, under the pure light of day, we shall light a holy flame in the depths of this pit. We will send these unfortunates down, down into the depths to face the demon which has cursed them. In doing so, we shall raise them up, up, all the way to salvation."

"Sir?" asked the sergeant, confused. "I'm sorry, sir, I don't understand. Are they going down or up?"

"I was speaking symbolically," said the Quæsitor. "The holy flame in the pit that consumes the demon will cleanse their souls as well and send them to heaven. Their bodies, regrettably, will not survive, but so it must be. Do you understand? Please make all necessary preparations."

"Um..." The sergeant was completely lost at this point. "You're going to clean them, sir? Should I get soap? Some brushes maybe?"

The Quæsitor now realized he had been speaking too abstractly. He sighed and spoke again, this time without any symbolism of any kind.

"No, not soap, sergeant – firewood. Lots and lots of firewood, enough to fill the bottom of that pit up to a man's waist. Add a barrel of pine resin as well and a half barrel of rock oil. Is that clear enough for you?" The sergeant saluted and wheeled about to carry out his order.

The Quæsitor turned toward the pit one last time, smiling with all his teeth, even the ones he took care to keep hidden. Kneeling down and putting his face over the edge, he spoke again, but this time in a low whisper, far too quiet for human ears to hear.

"Are you there, Ursine? I know you can hear me. It pains me to see such a mighty warrior come to such a sad end. Are you sure you wish to die this way? I did make you a different offer." He paused for a moment, but there was no reply, so he went on.

"Oh – and I should tell you, I know all about your mate and her..." he inhaled hungrily, "...condition. Does that change your mind?"

A distant owl hooted, abandoned scaffolding creaked in the wind, but from the pit there was only silence. The Quæsitor brushed a speck of dust from his boots and stood up.

"Still nothing to say? No? Very well. Enjoy your honorable death, *gharammir*. I certainly will!"

After he vanished, a soft rumble sounded from below and teeth gleamed in the darkness – very large teeth indeed. A huge shape retreated to the darkest corner of the pit and waited.

he hour that followed the Quæsitor's departure was tortuous. The mayor screamed until his throat was raw, crying out for his citizens to come and rescue their hero, the savior of Lünaborg. A few windows could be heard closing in the distance and a few of the lighter sleepers woke briefly. Some of them may have even felt a little guilty, but none of them came to help. He cried out for his loyal councilors to come to his aide, reminding them who had led them to glory.

"I gave you everything, you ingrates!" he shouted. "You'd all still be fighting each other for pennies, if it weren't for me. Your fortunes, your titles, all of it is because of me!"

He kept going on and on until one of the guard soldiers promised to give him the worst beating of his life if he didn't quiet down. When the prisoner stood up, chains shaking with fury and said "Do you know who I am?" the soldier followed through, exactly as promised. The beating went on for a long, long time. When it finally ended, the mayor's chain of office had been snatched from his neck and his elegant robes were torn from his body. He lay on the ground, too hurt and miserable to cry, shivering despite the warm night air. Eventually, the merchant took pity on him, helping him sit up and propping his bruised back against the post.

"How could they all abandon me?" he sniveled, very quietly. "I am their mayor, the most powerful person in Lünaborg!"

"No," whispered the merchant. "That's who you *were*."

Shocked, despite the pain he was in, the mayor stared at him blankly. "What?"

"You're not mayor and you're not powerful. Not anymore. Do you understand?"

And a friendless, broken man realized exactly who he had become;

a prisoner, condemned, despised, and abandoned, just a few hours from an agonizing death. His head sank down to his chest and he fell into a state of catatonic despair. The merchant started to speak again, thinking to offer a few words of empty comfort, but he was interrupted when, without warning, every single one of their guards fell asleep.

All around them, the soldiers who stood guard lost consciousness. Uniformed bodies slumped forward and long muskets toppled to the ground. Within moments, the air was filled with the sounds of snoring.

"They'll not hurt you again," said a deep voice from the pit below them. "They are having a nice sleep."

"Is this more of your sorcery, bear-thing?" the merchant replied. "Are these soldiers also victims of your evil spells?"

"It wasn't hard to do, they were already very tired. When they wake up, they will feel quite refreshed, as though they've woken from a lovely hibernation. Anyway, I'm saving your life," the voice said, a little peevishly. "A little gratitude wouldn't be amiss. I'm told that you humans set great store by politeness."

"We don't need your evil wiles," the merchant said, even though he thought it might be worth risking just a little evil and maybe one small wile if it meant he might live.

"Didn't your mother teach you any manners when you were a cub?" the voice joked. "You could say 'Thank you, bear! Thank you for saving me from being burned alive.' Go ahead. Take your time, I'll wait."

The merchant crawled over to the edge of the pit, dragging his chains with him so he could look straight down. Sure enough, the naked man stared up at him.

The voice teased, "Are you sure I'm not a demon?"

"Absolutely. Demons are smart. A demon would have the sense to appear as something more beguiling than you are. Or at least wear pants."

"What is that?" the former mayor whispered, roused from his internal contemplation. "What voice speaks?"

Now the naked man grinned from ear to ear. "Is that who I think it is?" he laughed aloud. "Hail to the conquering hero of Lünaborg! Hail to the man who single-handedly saved his city from my bloody rampage of death and destruction!"

"See, that's how I know you're not a demon," said the merchant, dryly. "No minion of darkness would be that irritating. I guess that his grace, the Quæsitor was mistaken."

At the mention of the Quæsitor, the man in the pit growled. "That one," he said, "is not what he seems."

"And I suppose you're going to tell me he is the demon?" said the merchant, curiously.

A grimly determined look came over the man who stood below him, who shook his head. "He's something worse than that."

"How could he be worse than a demon?" asked the merchant. "What is he?"

"That's a long story," said the naked man, "and there's no time left to explain." All traces of his teasing, playful manner vanished as he released all fear and doubt from his heart and willed himself to Change.

As the merchant and the former mayor watched in amazement, his barrel-chested frame grew larger, his limbs lengthened, and his muscles swelled. While the first traces of dawn tinged the eastern horizon, the interior of the pit was illuminated by a panorama of glittering stars. Soon, the figure in the center of the hole was no longer a man, but a great bear again, with eyes the color of a brilliant summer moon.

It spoke to the two men, in a soaring resonant roar only they could hear, a sound that was tragic and noble, honorable even as it surrendered to death. Within the vast darkness of his eyes, constellations flickered and spun.

"Hear me, little *ohusim* and heed my words. Soon, the deceiver, the one you call the Quæsitor will return to sacrifice us in a mockery of justice, calling it the will of the divine and the defense of freedom. He delights in such perversions, for his is a cult of pain that has been responsible for great atrocities; the slaughter of the wolf-men by human mobs, your own wars of religion, and the rise of insensate cruelty in the name of order."

"Why?" asked the merchant, perplexed. "Why would anyone wish for such things?"

"A desire to reverse past defeats; a desire fueled by a pure, cosmic arrogance. My, how this Quæsitor adores himself! I can feel him reveling in his own cleverness, even at this distance. But he will soon learn that even he is fallible. At sunrise, he will learn."

And the two men felt the contours of a future event form in their minds, imparting the shape of things to come. It was more than a vague premonition, but sharp and clear as a dream that is remembered upon waking. As it flowed into their consciousness, the mighty bear spoke again.

"Listen now and I will explain the part that you both shall play in my death..."

The crowds assembled at sunrise, pouring out of Lünaborg's gates, drawn by the calls of the town criers. An official writ hastily penned by the Quæsitor, had been easily approved at an emergency meeting of the city council only a few hours earlier. The remaining councilors had watched the figure dressed in dark, clotted red occupy the mayor's chair at the head of the table. All of them quickly came to an important realization – there was plenty of room in the pit for more bodies.

Observers familiar with the Lünaborg city council would have been amazed at the behavior of those attending the emergency meeting. No one attempted to subvert the vote for their own benefit, no last minute demands delayed the motion, and no one resorted to threats or blackmail to extract lucrative concessions. In an unprecedented show of unity, they voted unanimously and declared that this day was meant not for squabbling or petty gain but for rejoicing! At last, the great and terrible hell-bear would be executed, along with the two men who had fallen under its evil spell. In order to ensure that everyone rejoiced properly, they further declared it was required that everyone turn out to witness the Quæsitor's holy judgment, and that they should do so out of their own free will. A half-holiday from all work was declared[10] and anyone caught shirking this spontaneous, wholly voluntary celebration, they declared, would be lightly horsewhipped and severely fined.

They didn't really need to go to all the trouble of noble declarations and horsewhips. Most of the residents of Lünaborg would have come anyway. Free entertainment wasn't to be missed, and while hangings and beheadings happened fairly often, the roasting alive of criminals and hell-beasts did not – not since the last of the local werewolves had been publicly burned at the stake

---

[10]Unpaid, of course.

sixty years earlier. This would be an event to remember, particularly for all the children.

The captain of the militia rode up to oversee preparations, which was a challenging thing to do given that he was too scared to go anywhere near the pit. He had intended to make a grand pronouncement to open the proceedings, but all he managed was a strangled squeak before he turned his horse around, rode back to the regimental stables, and hid under a pile of straw. After he left, the council secretary climbed onto one of the scaffolds to address the crowd but he had a terrible voice for public speaking and his words were muffled by his beard, so hardly anyone heard him. No one listened anyway for there was too much excitement, too many shouts and jests, too many hawkers selling buns, ale, and roast apples, too many bets being placed on how long the fire would burn or how long it would take the hell-bear to die. When the poor council secretary finally stopped his attempt to read the charges against the mayor and the merchant, he tottered off the scaffold and nobody even noticed. The happy tumult continued for many more moments.

That changed once the Quæsitor appeared, stepping lightly up so everyone could see him. Everyone went immediately silent while the sweet, grandfatherly man explained that they would witness a remarkable event, the destruction of a creature of evil and the men it had corrupted. Then he ordered them to bow their heads while he led them all in prayer. Of the hundreds gathered there, only one listener knew that the language in which the Quæsitor made his recitation was not Latin, but something far more ancient. When he finished, he gave the order to light the fire. Torches were flung down and it did not take long for the resin and the oil to start burning. The sweet smoke drifted skyward and soon the depths of the pit could no longer be seen.

The crowd was packed in quite tightly at first, all struggling for a glimpse and pushing forward. As the fire started to grow, the soldiers forced the crowds away from the circumference of the pit, warning that the smoke

and heat would be intense as the many cords of wood went up in flames. As the spectators edged away, most of them could barely glimpse the two figures in chains being splashed with holy oil[11] and forced to their knees. The very top of a white-haired head framed by a high reddish collar could be seen for a moment, standing over the prisoners murmuring blessings and making passes with his hands. Despite craning necks and standing on tip-toe, the only ones who could see what transpired next were those lucky children who had an unobstructed view from their father's shoulders.

One small girl narrated the events to her family, captivated by the scene that unfolded in front of her.

"What's going on, *liebschen*?" her father asked from somewhere down near her knees. "Have the sinners been cast into the flames yet?"

"Not yet, papa!" she exclaimed. "The man with the red clothes is still talking to them."

"Is he poking them with red-hot pokers or putting splinters of

---

[11] While most Quæsitors considered whale oil to be the holiest of oils, as it caught easily and burned quickly, others felt olive oil was actually holier since it had a higher flash point, thereby allowing the condemned to cook slowly before going up in smoke.

wood under their fingernails?" asked the girl's mother, hopefully.

"No, but he is smiling a lot." She didn't know how to explain that the too-wide, too-white smile on the face of the man-in-red seemed much worse than pokers or splinters.

"What's happening now?" her brother asked, impatiently. He was angry because he was too big to ride on shoulders anymore. "What's the devil-bear doing?" he demanded.

"I can't see much of it," the girl said. "Just the tops of its ears. I think it's just sitting there still. The two men in chains, they are on their knees and people are throwing things at them now." The boy nodded at this, for it was traditional for the accused to receive appropriate mockery and a shower of rotten vegetables. The girl was surprised that while the little one in the rumpled nightshirt looked appropriately terrified, the taller one with the rough hands and the nice coat didn't seem bothered. He was staring back at the crowds in delight. She was too far away to hear him say to his doomed companion how nice it was to see such a fantastic audience at his arena, but the look on his face at the sight of working men and women having a nice time in his monument to mirth made her laugh. Her voice must have cut through the growing crackle of the flames and the murmur of the crowd, for she saw him look up at her and wink.

"Oh," she said suddenly, for the flames were burning higher now, sending up thick clouds of pale gray woodsmoke. There was a stir as the man-in-red turned to the sergeant-at-arms and ordered the prisoners be stood up and pushed backwards into the fire. "Here they go!" she shouted. Two soldiers came forward with sharp bayonets fixed at the ends of their muskets, intent on forcing the still-shackled prisoners into the rising smoke and down, down to the fire.

Oddly, she noticed that the man-in-red was not watching them, but looking beatifically around expectantly. A number of Quæsitor colleagues, the ones who had been hurriedly summoned to Lünaborg, took a step forward, anticipating a last minute rescue attempt.

"Wait," the girl announced, "they've stopped. Something's wrong."

The man-in-red had held up a spindly hand. His expression changed and she heard his voice calling out, "Well, where are you, bear-girl? This is your last chance to save your idiot husband! Soon the fire will be too hot, even for him." His sweet smile was subtly deformed now, turning into a rictus of impatient cruelty. "I know you're there. I can smell you, freak!" he shouted. "Come, let's see how true love conquers all! Show me that brave, indomitable spirit!"

Everything seemed to freeze at that moment and the girl on her father's shoulders realized she was holding her breath.

A woman in ordinary peasant garb broke the crowd's paralysis with a blur of motion. She seized the heads of the two soldiers who were busily forcing the prisoners into the flames, bringing their heads up with the force of her grip before banging their skulls together hard enough to knock them out. Not waiting for the limp soldiers to hit the ground, she had already grabbed the shackled arms of the prisoners and had snapped the iron bindings as if they were paper bracelets. With a swift jerk, she pulled the prisoners back from the edge of the pit, just as a blistering wave of heat rose from the earth. The fire burned furiously, sending up plumes of heat and clouds of smoke that started to blot out the rising sun.

Fast as she was, the Quæsitor was slightly faster. Before the little girl on her father's shoulders could blink, the Quæsitor leapt toward the peasant woman. His smile had grown so wide and so bright, it was blinding in the morning sun.

The only person in the crowd who had a good look was the little girl. She noticed that the man-in-red's teeth had gotten much longer and sharper, white as snow, but gnarled and uneven. Four other figures shoved their way towards the woman, converging like talons to seize and crush their prey. An unexpected sound rose up from the inferno that raged in the pit. The great bear did not cry out in pain nor did he roar as the fire finally overcame him. Instead, he sang with all his heart, weaving a song of inexpressible beauty.

As he burned, the great bear sang a song for the cub he would never have the chance to meet, and for all the children of all species, everywhere in the world who have ever been afraid, hungry, lonely, or frightened. Though his voice may have been strange and his language archaic, the meaning of his song was clear.

He sang to them that though this world was full of woe and want, it did not need to be so. He sang to them of a world that could be, of a future which was unwritten, and how the threads of fate might be severed. He sang the end of fear, the end of want. He sang them their dreams in verses that transcended words.

As the singing stopped, a great shower of sparks rose up out of the pit and the heat wafting from it increased tremendously. A rumble from deep underground was accompanied by a sudden tremor that shook the ground. "Earthquake!" someone cried out and a second tremor soon followed. The abandoned scaffolding released a shower of dust and the heavy blocks of stone that had been left in haphazard piles all about the building site wobbled

precariously. All thoughts of free entertainment and council decrees were forgotten as panic ensued and everyone tried to flee before the edge of the pit gave way.

The little girl was jostled as she sat on her father's shoulders, but he held her steady, fearing to put her down in the midst of the stampede, and ordered his son to hold tight to his belt. In the end, the girl was the only spectator who clearly witnessed what happened next; how the shorter prisoner - the former mayor - sooty and swaying, crashed right into the man-in-red who was lunging for the woman. The sad, broken little man's unexpected force surprised the Quæsitor, knocking him sideways off his feet, and sent him tumbling right into the pit.

Only the little girl witnessed the paws of the great bear reach from the flames to seize the Quæsitor, holding him in a fierce embrace. And she was the only one who witnessed the falling body of the man-in-red change to a twisted, wolf-like form, devoid of fur and covered with unwholesome scars. A pair of hellish red eyes met hers for a moment, just before they melted into the white-hot furnace of the pit.

That was all. The smoke grew too thick after that. The girl's mother didn't survive the panic, for she fell and was trampled underfoot. Her father kept his head, pushing through the maddened mass of people and dragging his children to safety.

The girl never told anyone all that she had seen and in the midst of the tragedy, for no one ever bothered to ask.

T he earthquake didn't last long and it was strangely localized, causing little damage in Lünaborg itself and only really affecting the building site outside the town. All that remained was a jumbled mess of shattered stone blocks and broken timbers. At its center sat the smoking crater where the bear's pit had once been. No one was inspired to dig through the rubble to hunt for salvage, not even to look for the mayor's chain of office or whatever might remain in the merchant's lost strongboxes.

Two nights after the incident, a soldier on guard spotted what he thought was a robed figure moving among the ruins, lifting up giant stones as though they weighed almost nothing and tossing aside scorching wreckage with hardly any effort. It seemed to be searching for something in the pit, and after a while it left carrying what appeared to be an unbelievably large skull. It bore the somber bones away with intense sorrow and reverence.

Since the soldier knew much better than to make a report about something that couldn't possibly have happened, he kept silent, and as time went on, he found many occasions to use this strategy.

He was eventually recognized by his officers as being unusually perceptive and keen and got promoted all the way to captain.

Epilogue

The two men who escaped the fires that day were never seen again. Patrols and search parties turned up nothing and eventually, the hunt was abandoned. The merchant and the mayor ceased to exist.

In an unrelated matter, a ship sailing out of Bremen took on two odd-looking sailors at the last minute before casting off for the English colonies across the sea. The captain had some concerns about the bedraggled looking pair, particularly the way they would periodically bicker about nothing at all.

Their habit of looking over their shoulders made it very clear to him that both were on the run from the law. He would have turned them away, but the tall one knew his way around a boat and the short one was oddly persuasive.

Despite their ragged, cast-off clothing and irritating tendency to argue with each other, he needed two more bodies and so he took a chance and signed them on as deckhands. He watched them go up the gangplank with mild regrets...

"Up you go, your lordship, don't trip on your robes of office," the tall one said, sarcastically.

"Quiet, you fool of a shopkeep," the short one snapped back, trying so hard to look unconcerned and innocent that it was extremely obvious he was guilty of something.

The captain shook his head and followed them up then busied himself with getting underway. He never noticed the cloaked, hooded woman standing on the quayside, silently watching as the ship cast off and sailed away on the morning tide.

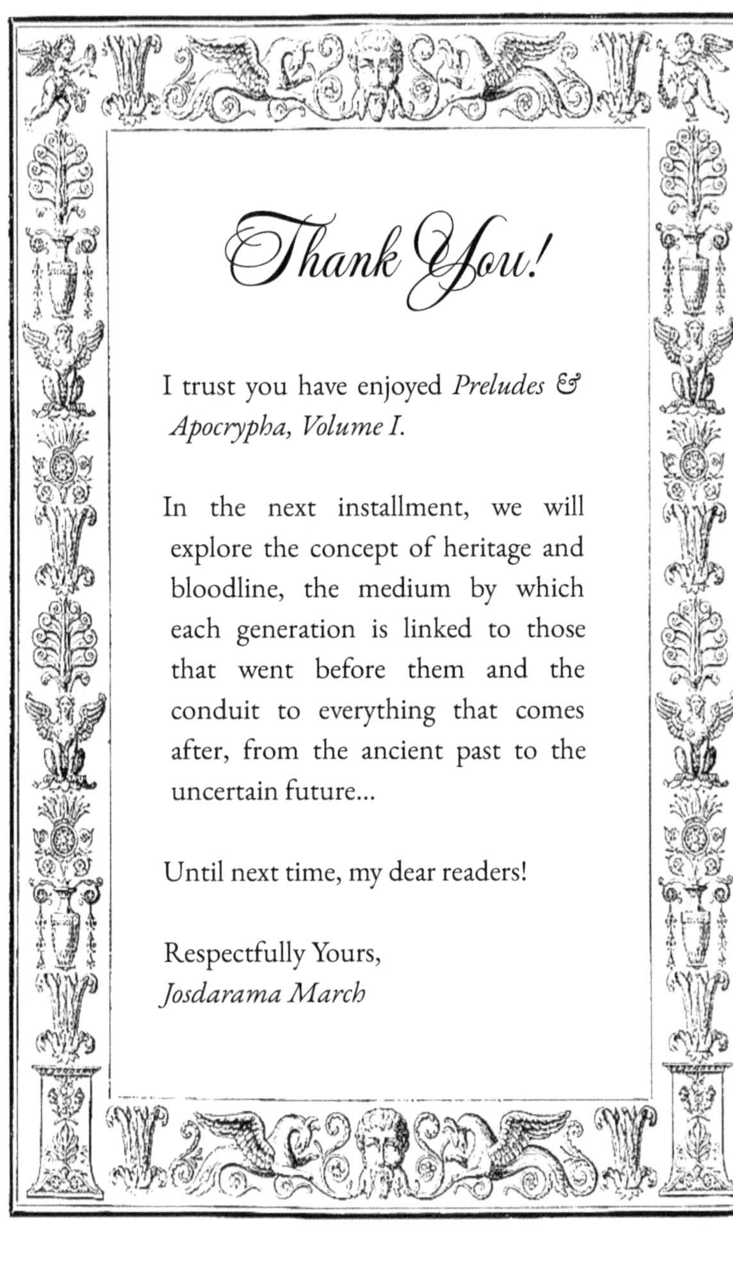

Thank You!

I trust you have enjoyed *Preludes &
Apocrypha, Volume I.*

In the next installment, we will
explore the concept of heritage and
bloodline, the medium by which
each generation is linked to those
that went before them and the
conduit to everything that comes
after, from the ancient past to the
uncertain future...

Until next time, my dear readers!

Respectfully Yours,
Josdarama March

Coming Soon:
Preludes & Apocrypha
Vol. II
Bloodlines

January 17th, 1907

To Our Valued Customers:

Three months ago, my father, Charles Octavius, Sr. passed away. While his death was sudden and unexpected, I and my family took comfort in the fact that his memory would live on at Octavius & Sons, Inc. (*est.* 1765) as part of our company's legacy.

Unfortunately, while his memory may live on, our company will not. It pains me great to inform you that after four generations of love and labor, we are closing shop for good.

The financial losses from our recent publications, particularly *Preludes & Apocrypha*, and the subsequent withdrawal of our lines of credit have forced us to declare bankruptcy. Our board has been forced to sell what little remains of the business to ABYSSAL HOLDINGS, INC. (a wholly-owned subsidiary of LENNOX CONSORTIUM, LTD.)

Now, our new owners have asked that we kindly note the following:

☞ All of our magazines, journals and periodicals, including *Preludes & Apocrypha* will cease publication immediately.

☞ All future subscriptions are hereby canceled and unsold copies (particularly *Preludes & Apocrypha*) are to be returned for disposal.

☞ All complaints and refund requests may be sent to: Abyssal Holdings, *Attn.* Refunds & Incinerations

I thank all of you for being loyal customers and subscribers of Octavius & Sons (*est.* 1765) and I wish you all the best in the years to come.

Sincerely,

Charles Octavius, Jr.

Publisher & Chairman, Ex-Officio

FINIS.

Sign Up for Special Offers &
The Latest Updates At:
www.varsityaesthetics.com
www.littlewerewomen.com